P

"Just like *The Communist* ... a funny sexy violent storyline. Wish I'da thought of that."

–Karl Marx, author of
The Communist Manifesto

"Mouse, Bear and Elephant Games is the ultimate realpolitik fantasy. It's like *Game of Thrones* meets *House of Cards*, complete with villains, conmen, schemers and dreamers. You'll recognize the characters immediately. You will love some, and hate others, but you won't be able to put this book down. It's addictive reading and forces us to consider some uncomfortable truths about our world today. This book is a powerful and stunning achievement. Don't miss it."

–*Realpolitik Book Review*

"The cover made me think it's a good book for children. It is not…I feel cheated, and I'd like my money back!"

–Beatrice Patter, beloved author of
The Fuzzy Wuzzy Books

"Of all those writers working in the grand speculative fantasy field, Piper is by far the best. What really marks his books as revolutionary is the author's refusal to see the world as merely a biblical struggle between good and evil. Piper's characters are regular everyday people that you know, just writ larger. They are funny or tragic, or tragically funny, and brutally honest or honestly brutal, and somehow that makes them mean more. Some are heroes, some cowards, some are filled with love and hope, others still with hate and betrayal. These characters, like ourselves, are slugging it out in muck pits, one day at a time, for love and money and lust and power. Unless you don't slug things out in muck pits, or crave money and love and power. And if you don't do any of those things, how do you even live with yourself? I mean, do you pay someone else to fight your battles in muck pits for you? Put this book down immediately, you bourgeois capitalist…"

–Richard Head, *Muck pit Magazine*

"A totally ridiculous fantasy explaining how our planet might be saved from extinction brought about by corporate and personal greed. But it's just a fantasy. We won't let these ideas happen. Back to work, drones."

-Rich Old White Men Everywhere

"This is a dangerous book and threatens to shake the very foundations on which American freedom was established. It's a thinly veiled blueprint for the next revolution. The author should be imprisoned, far away from pen and ink, or, better yet, hanged for treason."

–Joseph McCarthy

"The best Trimpanzombie apocalypse survival guide ever written."

–Fidel Castro

@realDonaldTrimp: Lyin' Mark Piper has written another terrible, I mean, just the worst, book about me. FAKE NEWS! There was no covfefe, and I never touched that woman. I will sue everyone who buys this book. I have the best lawyers!

–Donald J. Trimp, 45th POTUS

To Dusty:

Mouse, Bear and Elephant Games

Viva la Revolucion!! :)

Always and always

MARK PIPER

M.S. Piper
a local Dartmouth Feller

Mouse, Bear and Elephant Games
Copyright © 2018 by Mark Piper

All rights reserved. No part of this publication may be reproduced, distributed, or transmitted in any form or by any means, including photocopying, recording, or other electronic or mechanical methods, without the prior written permission of the author, except in the case of brief quotations embodied in critical reviews and certain other non-commercial uses permitted by copyright law.

Tellwell Talent
www.tellwell.ca

ISBN
978-0-2288-0691-2 (Hardcover)
978-0-2288-0690-5 (Paperback)
978-0-2288-0692-9 (eBook)

Table of Contents

Foreword ix
Preface xi
Acknowledgements. xiii

Chapter 1: The Lights are On, But... 1
Chapter 2: The 46th POTUS. 17
Chapter 3: Canadiana Special 27
Chapter 4: Yay, Daddy's Home! 51
Chapter 5: Jets or Bush Planes?. 62
Chapter 6: Viva la Resistance!. 76
Chapter 7: Your Grampa Had
           the Biggest Wacek. 87
Chapter 8: Dark Days and Darker Nights 100
Chapter 9: Some Radical Proposals 110
Chapter 10: Control the Media,
            Control the Message 124
Chapter 11: The Shittiest Chapter 141
Chapter 12: The Russian Bear Rises. 153
Chapter 13: To Get Ahead, We
            Must Go Backwards 164

Chapter 14: "MAGA, Then KAG" 174

Chapter 15: Spring Break 188

Chapter 16: "This Is Not A Drill" 200

Chapter 17: "Keep Your F$#&ing
               Thoughts and Prayers…" 215

About the Author 233

Foreword

By Vladimir Poutine
President of the Russian Federation

Unknown Canadian author sends Vladimir book, asks Vladimir to write foreword as geo-political expert and maniacal strongman. Vladimir refuses, is busy.

Author tells Vladimir book is filled with sexy-sexy boom-boom political intrigue. Author also tells Vladimir book makes Vladimir look like strong, sexy world leader. Vladimir refuses, is too busy.

Author is persistent, sends tape of Vladimir doing boom-boom to Donald Trimp.

Tape is fuzzy, Trimp lover identity is clearly not Vladimir. Lawyers suggest easier and safer to write foreword, just in case. So—under protest—Vladimir writes foreword.

Mouse, Bear and Elephant Games author is liar. Book is not so much sexy-sexy and very little boom-boom. Well, maybe some boom-boom when Vladimir is in story. First problem with book. Not enough Vladimir.

Ideas in book is not possible. Author is maybe sick in head or drug freak? Book says not true bad things about Donald Trimp. Book has crazy dreams about honest politicians and saving planet from greedy people. Vladimir laughs with maniacal strongman laughter. Two things not possible.

Book is written in "near crazy alternate future" in stupid "not true world" where Vladimir and Donald Trimp do bad things. Vladimir and Donald Trimp would never do bad stupid things in book.

Book is full of stupid, but Vladimir likes parts where Canadian prime minister makes boom-boom with sexy politician girlfriend, and where Melanie Trimp dreams of boom-boom with Canadian prime minister. And any other parts of book where people make boom-boom and drink *krupnik*. Also, funny part about man with big *wacek*, because Vladimir has big *wacek*. Writer probably meant story to be about Vladimir's *wacek*. That would be great book.

But mostly, book is full of stupid hope and not real dreams. People should not read. Vladimir will write better book soon, about Vladimir's triumphs in world with sexy-sexy big *wacek*.

There. Stupid foreword written. Vladimir never promised good foreword. Now, Mark Piper, burn boom-boom Trimp tape. No…second thinking. Send to Vladimir. I might need to strongman Donald Trimp.

Preface

Mouse, Bear and Elephant Games

Thank you, Mr. Poutine. You are highly regarded in the "maniacal strongman" category of world leaders, so your critical review and foreword for *Mouse, Bear and Elephant Games* is deeply appreciated.

As with *The Mouse Who Poked an Elephant*, I have tried to write a book that provides alternate options to us in the near future. Baby boomers will likely think some of the changes discussed in this series of books are unsettling, uncomfortable, unnecessary or downright ridiculous. I get it. Nobody likes change, especially if we are comfortable and well off. Wealthy baby boomers in the G7 or G20 countries need to admit that our planet can't continue to support the lifestyles we want, at least not without a lot of other people suffering to pay for it. FYI, baby boomers in the G7 countries have 90 per cent of the world's wealth and wield incredible power. Essentially, our generation has raped the planet's resources for profit, while somehow simultaneously racking up record levels of personal and national debt.

Can we change our political, economical and environmental systems to share the planet's resources more equitably? If we intend to change our ways we should start soon. The alternative is to be remembered as the generation that was too greedy, short-sighted and arrogant to change and instead left our children's children a planet too exploited and polluted to support life. So, this story is a light-hearted look at how those changes could happen.

This story is a work of fiction. Characters resembling real people you may know is purely coincidence.

Mark Piper
October 2018

Acknowledgements

As is often the case, none of this would have been possible without the endless love and support of my family. Much thanks and love to my wife Elaine for encouraging me to follow my dreams.

Our sons Brechin and Brendan inspired many of the optimistic alternatives to our current status quo discussed in this book. *Mouse, Bear and Elephant Games* is dedicated to them, their generation and anyone else courageous enough to admit we need to change.

You know how people sometimes say: "Don't judge a book by its cover?" Well, none of the people who say that have ever written, then independently published books. So, a big shout out to Keith MacLeod of Dartmouth, Nova Scotia, for crushing the cover art.

Books (good ones, at least) aren't possible without the watchful eyes of editors. Thanks for your patience, JoAnn Alberstat.

Last but never least, endless gratitude to the team at Tellwell Publishing for helping this author through the publishing process.

Canadians and the Canadian government have always placed tremendous importance on our relationship with the United States. After all, they are the only neighbour with whom we share a border. Former Canadian Prime Minister Pierre Trudel used the analogy of a mouse sleeping with an elephant in describing the relationship between the two nations while speaking to the Washington Press Club in 1971.

"While the United States does not have to be overly concerned about the Canadian mouse, the mouse—no matter how friendly and even-tempered the elephant— must be affected by its every twitch and grunt."

@realDonaldTrimp: Actually, throughout my life, my two greatest assets have been mental stability and being, like, really smart. I went from VERY successful businessman, to top T.V. Star, to President of the United States (on my first try). I think that would qualify as not smart, but genius… and a very stable genius at that! 9:30 AM - Jan 6, 2018

CHAPTER 1

The Lights are On, But...

Washington DC

"Gotta launch now!

Gotta launch now!

Gotta launch now!" Donald J. Trimp kept repeating angrily, hammering on his phone. As doctors, nurses and orderlies attempted to take his blood pressure, he clumsily punched a nurse in the back of the neck. It was, of course, the lead story on every news channel in the world. The final footage showed orderlies sedating the former president with an injection and putting him in restraints.

"That was exclusive footage of former President Trimp from an anonymous source at Walter Reed Medical Center," Megan Kellye, the NBC announcer, explained. "Our next story covers the heroic work being done by medical personnel in the aftermath of the 'Great Canadian Blackout...'"

All of Washington DC's hospitals were overflowing with the wounded and dying from the recent violent demonstration during the blackout. An estimated 1,200 American citizens had been killed by various US security forces during the protest. Additionally, there were approximately 6,000 personnel wounded and another 15,000 people were incarcerated in jails and military bases in the greater capital area.

For many people in America, the past three years had been a frightening time to be alive. Very few people wanted to be caught saying or listening to anything that criticized President Trimp. Trimp's relentless attacks on the "fake news" media since his election had ultimately resulted in random Trimpanzees harassing and molesting any newspersons or individuals who criticized the POTUS.

Throughout the 20th century, people got their news first from newspapers, then from the radio, then later through television sets. Regardless of the medium–print, radio or television–most reporters and journalists were generally regarded as people who were trained and educated to observe facts and report on those facts.

Rapid technological advances had changed all that. By 2010, anyone with a cellphone or i-Pad could record events and tweet opinions to a large audience. Current events became less about correctly reporting facts and more about editorial opinion pieces. American media outlets were more clearly and easily identified as "right" or "left" leaning. By 2020, it was difficult to identify a media platform that was not perceived as biased. All the Democrats seemed to hate or mistrust Fox News or Breitbart, and all the Republicans believed only Fox, Breitbart or President Trimp's tweets. The sheer amount of misinformation available on any topic was staggering. Nevertheless, there were still some people who had trained to be journalists and reporters practising their trade.

What journalists feared even more than harassment from random Trimpanzees was a visit by Trimp's own private security forces. "Team America" had been formed to counter the deep state. You see, Donald Trimp had always believed that deep state forces in the dark bowels of government were working hard to countermand and delegitimize his presidency.

Team America was spawned in 2018 as Trimp could no longer listen to anyone who criticized or questioned his decisions or legitimacy. Remember, Donald Trimp had never been criticized, prior to 2016, by anyone he couldn't fire. The First Amendment during Trimp's presidency was constantly being threatened. Those choosing to exercise freedom of speech did so at the risk of online or personal physical harassment from loyal Trimpanzees, or worse: an actual visit from the professional goons known as Team America.

Stanstead, Quebec

Meanwhile, just across the border, most Canadians were busy helping out their American neighbors who had arrived during the recent interruption of electrical power and natural gas to the US. Canadian militia members, fire and police services, and all levels of government were coordinating efforts as best they could. By midday on January 23 it was estimated that 1.7 million Americans had crossed the world's longest border. Although the actual blackout only lasted 48 hours, many Americans didn't seem to be in a hurry to return home. Visitors were being housed and fed in school gymnasiums, arenas, public buildings, armories and private homes.

The Canadian Red Cross was receiving record-shattering levels of donations for this latest relief effort. Bill Bates and his wife Belinda each donated $5 million from their new home in Vancouver to get the party started. Melanie Trimp donated $3 million (on behalf of Mr. Trimp) while the Cliftons, Oobimas and G.W. Busches gave $2 million each.

That trio of former presidents and their wives took it a step further. Mallory and Bill Clifton were volunteering at the Haskell Free Library and Opera House. The beautiful neo-classical limestone building sits directly on the border between Stanstead, Quebec, and Derby Line, Vermont.

"As far as I know, this is the only library in the world that operates in two countries," Mallory Clifton stated to reporters. "And we're certainly very grateful to our Canadian hosts at this point in our history."

"Mrs. Clifton, will you comment on President Trimp's attempted nuclear launch on Canada?" an ABC reporter asked.

"Well, I'm grateful that our Joint Chiefs of Staff had the foresight and good sense not to give him nuclear codes," she replied defiantly.

"Mrs. Clinton, how do you feel now that President Trimp has been arrested?" another reporter wondered.

"Especially considering the 'Lock Her Up!' chants at Republican rallies?" another voice asked from the crowd.

"Honestly, I do feel safer with that man not being our president," Mallory Clifton replied sadly. "Our country has been broken and divided during Trimp's reign of terror.

I'm confident that Nancy Pillosi will do a tremendous job as president, until the election this November."

"Mrs. Clifton, will you be running in the Democratic primary later this year?" a young female journalist shouted over her colleagues. The room got quieter. This was what they really came to hear.

"I took my shot in 2016," Mallory Clifton deadpanned. "I think you all know how that worked out. I'm willing to help with the election as a volunteer in some capacity, but I won't be running in the primary."

The reporters were clamoring and shouting more questions at the former secretary of state, but a small group of security personnel led her to another room. Her husband, the former president, switched the topic as smoothly as possible.

"Tonight, there's a jamboree and singalong in the Opera House upstairs, with donations being collected for the Canadian Red Cross relief efforts," President Clifton stated cheerfully. "The stage is in Canada and the audience is in the USA. And everyone is welcome, no matter where they are from."

"Will you be playing your saxophone tonight, Mr. President?" a reporter wanted to know.

"I'm pretty rusty," President Clifton laughed. "But we'll see how the show goes."

St. Stephen, New Brunswick

Just across the Maine border there was a big lobster dinner going down at the local Legion. Former President George W. Busch and the former first lady were serving up boiled lobster as fast as the boys in the back room could cook them. The mayor of St. Stephen used to caddy at a golf course in Kennebunkport, and he was showing the Buschs and a CBC reporter a black and white photo of himself with George Busch Sr, Dubya and Jeb. The picture was from 1963.

"Your dad used to ask for me as a caddy, and then he'd insist that I play along with you guys."

The Busch Family had managed thus far to keep their presence in New Brunswick fairly quiet. The single reporter from the CBC had quite a time covering the story.

"Mr. Mayor, was President Busch a good golfer?"

"Well, their dad was pretty good, but I think politics was the right career choice over golf for all three of them." The small circle of people around the Buschs and the mayor laughed politely.

"Mr. Busch, do you have a comment regarding Mr. Trimp's arrest?" the reporter continued.

"I'm saddened by it," the former president responded quietly. "As a Republican, I'm deeply embarrassed that our Grand Old Party has sunk to such depths." He paused for a minute to gather his thoughts, then spoke again, more vigorously, more optimistically. "But at the same time, I'm hopeful for America. I'm hopeful that this point in our history is the lowest we go, because if this is the bottom, we have nowhere to go but up."

The circle of people around the former president applauded politely. From the back kitchen, two older men were bringing out a large steaming pot of lobsters.

"Now, if you'll excuse me?" President Busch asked the reporter. "I have a group of hungry people to serve here."

The applause was louder this time, especially from the people waiting in line to be fed.

Buffalo Point, Manitoba

Further west, President Oobima, Michelle, Malia and Sasha were helping out at Buffalo Point First Nation on the border of Manitoba and Minnesota. "We have a population of 42 people, and by our count today we are housing 643 guests," the band chief Louise Riel proclaimed proudly for a group of reporters from Minneapolis and Winnipeg.

"Is it true that the Oobimas are staying here and helping out?"

"How will you be able to feed so many guests?"

"Can we meet the Oobimas?"

"OK, OK. First, come this way," Chief Riel gestured, crossing the lobby and opening the door to a large kitchen. Inside the kitchen the three Oobima girls were laughing and making bannock under the watchful eyes of several elderly Indigenous women.

"Mrs. Oobima, will you be running in the Democratic primary? A lot of Americans believe that you'd make a tremendous president."

Michelle smiled. "I'm not ruling anything out. I'm sure there will be plenty of exceptional candidates–from all sides–Democrat, Republican, Independent. I have faith that Americans will elect the president they believe will do the best job."

"Mrs. Oobima. where is your husband?" a reporter asked.

"Dress warm," she replied. "He's out fishing."

"Mrs. Oobima, would you comment on President Trimp's recent arrest?"

The former FLOTUS kept her expression neutral. "No comment."

Reporters were clamoring to ask more questions, but one of the older Buffalo Point women gently directed the press towards the door. "We got bannock to make."

After a few moments they resumed their questions, this time to the former POTUS.

"President Oobima, how are you enjoying Manitoba?"

"Well, it's beautiful here, but it's way colder than Kenya."

You could hear a pin drop for a second. "Awe, I'm just messing with y'all," he laughed. "I haven't been back to Kenya in years, and I certainly wasn't born there. Look, so far today I think I've caught the biggest fish." He held up a good-sized walleye, as the other folks in the ice fishing hut laughed politely.

They laughed louder when a boy about three feet tall held up a lake trout that was almost as big as the child himself.

"Can we get a comment on President Trimp's arrest?"

"And his attempt to launch nuclear weapons at Canada?"

The former president held up his hands, palms open. "Let me just say that I'm praying for all of the people in America today—and that includes Mr. Trimp and Vice President Pens and our new interim President, Nancy Pillosi. America has been going through a rough patch, but we'll get through this. And I want to express our thanks to the wonderful people all across Canada. We're very fortunate to share a border with the Canadian people. And I'll leave it there. That's all I have to say."

The press was clamoring for Mr. Oobima to take more questions, but Louise gently ushered them out of the fishing hut.

"Chief, how do you feel about having so many American visitors here today?"

"Everyone is welcome," Chief Riel replied gently. "Our ancestors didn't worry about these imaginary lines we call borders. We are all children of the Great Mother here."

Niagara Falls, Ontario

Similar relief centres and command posts (without the star power and cumbersome security teams that accompanied former presidents) had been set up in almost every town in Canada: in armories, high schools, churches, heated warehouses, public buildings–anywhere with heat that could be set up with cots.

Canada's recently expanded militia now stood at nearly 900,000 soldiers, sailors and air force personnel. T-Bone Brown and Lumpy Halerewich were a good example of the many young Canadians who had been reluctantly drafted into the militia, and now found themselves loving it.

"Thank you so much for your kindness," a beautiful young lady with a Latino accent said to Lumpy as he handed her a steaming bowl of soup.

Lumpy smiled and blushed. He and an older Latino lady who insisted on helping were serving a big crowd in the armory. "You're wel...welcome," Lumpy stuttered clumsily. After some time, the Latino lady cleared her throat with an obvious "ahem" and elbowed Lumpy to get his attention.

"You should go talk at that girl." As Lumpy began to protest, the lady stopped him, and held her hand out for the soup ladle.

"Her name is Fabiola."

Lumpy looked confused. "I'm her *abuela*," the lady explained. "*Madre de Dios*, take soup and go sit with her."

While Lumpy and Fabiola chatted shyly, two soldiers rolled in a big screen TV, and turned it on.

A tiny female soldier blew a loud whistle, and without speaking, pointed to the screen like a game show hostess. The Canadian prime minister skated onto the screen.

"Hi folks. Elijah here. Just getting my skate on with Juliette and some of our new friends." Elijah gestured to the crowd as the camera pulled back to show thousands of people skating on the Rideau Canal, with the Parliament Buildings in the background. It was a clear, crisp, cold night in Ottawa. Viewers could see the puff of everyone's breath as they exhaled. The PM and his girlfriend, the minister of youth, were both sporting Hudson's Bay winter jackets and matching 1970s-size Afros.

"That's the leader of your country?" Fabiola whispered to Lumpy. Lumpy nodded, and Fabiola smiled. "Who's *la chica* with him?"

"That's his girlfriend Juliette. She's a politician as well," Lumpy managed to say. He wasn't accustomed to speaking to beautiful, mysterious girls.

"I think I'm gonna love Canada," Fabiola responded sweetly.

The camera panned back in on Elijah. "So, two quick things we want to tell you. First, if you are visiting here, you don't have to go right away. We understand if you have things—family, a home, a job—that you need to return to. But, if you think you'd like to live here, you probably can. We are accepting applications for immigration at www.gc.ca/Newcomers/Services.

We'll do our best to process your applications as quickly as possible. If you're already here in Canada, you're welcome to hang out here with us while you consider your options. Now, I'll let Juliette tell you the second thing."

Juliette Sparks was beaming. "Hi, Mom. Hi, Canada. Hi, new friends. Just wanna put the rumors to rest. Yes, we're pregnant!" The crowd that had gathered around Elijah and Juliette cheered lustily. They went suddenly quiet as Elijah dropped to one knee facing Juliette.

"Actually, I guess there is another thing I need to ask." Elijah had never appeared nervous in anyone's recent memory, but he seemed a little shaky now. "Juliette, baby, I have been breathless since the day we met. I mean I can't breathe when I see you, but then, I can't breathe when we're apart. And I can't imagine a life without you. So please say that you'll marry me," he gushed. Elijah looked like he was about to faint. The crowd behind them on the Rideau Canal went quiet anticipating Juliette's answer.

She didn't make her boyfriend suffer too long. Juliette managed to squeak out an audible "Yes" between her tears of joy. Now the crowd went crazy. The folks skating on the Rideau Canal were going wild cheering, and there were big hoots and hollers of joy from the TV watchers in the armory as well.

A tiny oriental sergeant major whose name tag read "Lee" turned down the volume and addressed the crowd in the armory.

"Hmmm, I did not see that coming," she said in a surprised tone. The crowd tittered and chuckled. "OK, so that was unexpected and ridiculously romantic." Then she shook her head slightly and switched back into sergeant major mode. "But let's get back to business. You have some options tonight. Obviously, as it's always been, you are free to return home. We just ask that you notify us in the Administration room by the door—right where you signed in with us yesterday or the day before.

Or, if you want to stay, you can watch television here. We have a movie room upstairs with some family films, or if you'd prefer to sleep, you know where your bunks are."

She paused while Pte. T-Bone Brown whispered quietly in her ear. "And if you would prefer a more intimate setting, we still have private homes nearby that are welcoming guests. Talk to Private Halerewich…Halerewich, where are you? Put your hand up."

Lumpy raised his hand obediently.

"As I was saying, talk to Private Halerewich here if you are interested. He has a list of people willing to let you stay with them. Now, if you are hungry, there's a bottomless pot of chili in the kitchen, rolls, butter, tea, coffee, water, fruit, et cetera. Any questions?"

Within a few minutes the 200 visiting Americans had found something to do or were planning to leave. There were 142 people who decided they needed to leave—to check on their homes and return to work. The other 58 people were undecided and talked among themselves in small groups.

T-Bone was pushing his buddy Lumpy over to Fabiola, who had rejoined her grandmother and what appeared to be more of her family.

Fabiola spoke quickly in Spanish to her family. All he could make out was "*Soldero* Lumpy." She then introduced Lumpy to her father, Guillermo Gonzalez, and her brother Valariano. "And you already met *mi abuela*, Rosa Gonzalez," Fabiola added quickly.

Lumpy looked confused. "Umm, I thought she was like your grandmother?"

"Lumpy, *mi abuela* means 'my grandmother' *en espagnol*," Fabiola explained happily.

"It's a pleasure to meet you," he managed to say to them.

"*Mucho gusto*," the Gonzalez Family replied in unison.

Lumpy was looking awkwardly at his shoes when T-Bone nudged him again.

"Umm, Fabiola, if your family wants to stay at my grandmother's house, you can. I mean, it's not fancy or anything, but it's big and has a little more privacy than an armory. Just ahhhh…puttin' it out there as an option for you."

Fabiola spoke in rapid-fire Spanish to her father for a minute. The grandmother and brother also got into the conversation. The conversation seemed to be getting heated, arms and hands were flying, and wild gestures being made when the grandmother apparently put her foot down.

"My grandmother says we accept your offer, but you must let us pay your grandmother for the room," Fabiola smiled at Lumpy.

"Well, you don't have to, but…"

"Ah, but we must insist," Fabiola's grandmother interjected.

"If no paying, no staying," Fabiola's father added emphatically.

"My own gramma taught me never to argue or disagree with anybody's grandmother, so you are not gonna get any fight from me on this one," Lumpy laughed, raising his hands in mock surrender.

"I would like to know your grandmother," Rosa added.

"Well, you can meet her tonight, Ma'am. T-Bone and I rent rooms in her old house. Without renting rooms, she would have lost her house a few years back."

The armory was emptying out. The people staying for the night were getting ready for bed, and the oncoming shift of nine militia soldiers were getting briefed by Sgt.-Maj. Lee. "Well, we should get going," Lumpy suggested, checking his watch. "Our bus comes in five minutes. Do you need a minute to gather your things, or...?"

"We are good to go, aren't we, Gramma?"

"*Si, chica.*"

Lumpy and T-Bone insisted on taking the ladies' bags. "And we just need to stop here, and have you sign out," Lumpy directed as they approached the Administration office.

"Brown and Halerewich!" Sgt.-Maj. Lee snapped at the two privates, who snapped to attention. "Please tell me that your intentions with this family are as pure as the driven snow!" Sgt.-Maj. Lee had a voice like a whip cracking. It commanded respect.

"Yes, Sergeant Major," the two responded smartly, almost simultaneously.

"And are you escorting these folks to your grandmother's house, Private Halerewich?"

"Yes, Sergeant Major."

"Well, very good. They'll be happy there. Stand at... ease!" the tiny sergeant major barked at the two soldiers.

Her tone became warm and friendly as she addressed the ladies. "I trust that you enjoyed your stay here in our armory?" Fabiola assured the sergeant major that everything had been wonderful, and added translated compliments provided by her family on how helpful everyone had been, and how polite and professional her soldiers were.

"Well, we do our best to train them right, but it's a work in progress every minute of every day," the sergeant major sighed. "But don't worry about these two. They're pretty harmless. Enjoy the rest of your stay. It was nice to meet you."

The sergeant major shook hands with the Gonzalez Family, wheeled and marched smartly out of the room to straighten out a few more of her soldiers.

"I am liking your boss woman, *Soldero* Lumpy. She's funny," the elder lady said on the way to the car.

"Yeah, I guess?" Lumpy seemed puzzled by that statement. "My grandmother said the same thing about her. But me? I just find the sergeant major scary."

The old woman laughed gently at this. "Ahhh, some little fear and respect for authority people is healthy thing."

Democracy, nevertheless must not be disgraced. Democracy must not be despised. Democracy must be respected. Democracy must be honoured. Democracy must be cherished. Democracy must be an essential, an integral part of the Sovereignty, and have a control over the whole Government, or moral Liberty cannot exist, or any other Liberty.
—John Adams, Letter to John Taylor, Dec., 12. 1814

CHAPTER 2

The 46th POTUS

Washington DC

Hard-core Trimpanzees and loyal members of Cult 45 could not have seen this coming. It was a Republican's worst nightmare. Nancy Pillosi, a long-serving Democrat congresswoman and two-time House speaker, was the 46th president of the United States of America.

In accordance with the American Constitution, if the president of the United States is unable to fulfill their duties and responsibilities, the vice president assumes the presidency. However, in the unusual winter of 2020, Vice President Mike Pens was in a coma, courtesy of an uppercut from a Marine who lost his patience with the VP during the Great Canadian Blackout in January 2020. The next person in the line of succession is the speaker of the House of Representatives. The Democrats had won that House in the November 2018 midterm elections.

Nancy Pillosi was a very experienced and focused politician. Despite the sudden speed with which she had been elevated from House speaker to the presidency, she was quickly forming a competent staff in the White House.

She was currently receiving a nuclear launch briefing from the Joint Chiefs of Staff. They had covered sequence of launch and likely scenarios in which a nuclear launch might be a possibility. But there was a serious question she had to ask to the chairman.

"Admiral, three days ago, President Trimp, acting as our commander in chief, tried to launch a nuclear attack on Canada."

The senior officers looked at each other stonily as President Pillosi continued speaking. "Through the clear lens of hindsight, it now seems prudent that President Trimp was never given the correct launch codes. However, we can't overlook the fact that, as a group, the Joint Chiefs of Staff lied to and willingly misled the president of the United States. Going forward, how am I supposed to trust that what we have discussed in this briefing is true and factual?"

The chairman of the Joint Chiefs was about to answer, but the newly appointed president held up one finger. "I'll make it easier for you to answer. Do I, as the commander in chief of the United States, currently have the ability to launch nuclear weapons should they be required?"

Adm. McHale was the senior officer of the group and answered the question as chairman of the Joint Chiefs. "Madame President, let me assure you, you most certainly do have the ability to launch ICBMs. And, as a group, we have discussed our betrayal of President Trimp. It was distasteful to consider, but, in all of our opinions, it was the correct thing to do in 2016. President Trimp's recent attempt to launch our arsenal proved our darkest fears correct. It's important that you know this, Ma'am," McHale continued. "When we briefed President Trimp on this launch sequence in 2016, he seemed genuinely excited that he could wield such power. And that made us quite nervous. At some point had we genuinely needed to defend our country with nuclear weapons, we could have." Admiral McHale paused. "General Pruitt, you look like you have something to add to this?"

"Pit Bull" Pruitt was the senior Army officer present. He had clearly been Donald Trimp's favourite officer of the Joint Chiefs. The feeling had never been mutual. Nevertheless, President Trimp had often boastfully tweeted about the camaraderie that (he believed) the two shared.

There were multiple tweets like this one:

> *@realDonaldTrimp spent the day with 'Pit Bull' Pruitt touring Fort Benning and addressing our tremendous troops. The greatest President ever and the greatest military in the world. Together we will MAGA!*

Like many tweets from the POTUS, this was followed by 6,000 to 10,0000 comments, about 70 per cent of which were negative, and 30 per cent supportive.

"Pit Bull" Pruitt was six feet, four inches tall. He did triathlons to relax in his spare time and was a keen student of Muay Thai and Brazilian jiu-jitsu. His closely shaved head and jaw seemed entirely square, as if he were a human battering ram. His eyes were a cold, grey blue. He was a highly trained, stone-cold killing machine. He was also famous for getting right to the point.

"Madame President, I'm sure you are aware that each member of the Armed Services swears an oath to defend the Constitution of the United States from enemies, both foreign and domestic. Personally, I viewed Mr. Trimp as a domestic enemy. I tell you this so you understand why he was never given nuclear codes. Donald Trimp had the intellect and temperament of an eight-year-old bully. I honestly considered killing him with my bare hands every time we met, but especially when he tweeted photos of us together. I believe history would have forgiven me if I had killed him. I take cold comfort in the fact that he will now finally be judged for his many crimes. It's unfortunate and embarrassing that he was ever elected to a position of such immense power."

The rest of the room smiled wryly at General Pruitt's comments. "President Pillosi, there is one final point to consider," Adm. McHale continued. "Four years ago, as the Joint Chiefs of Staff, we knowingly and willfully colluded, lied to and misled the president of the United States, based on what we felt about the man's mental capacity, or lack thereof, to diligently discharge his duties as commander in chief. Ma'am, notwithstanding our reasons for what we did, the charge for that crime is treason. And those persons found guilty of treason may be awarded capital punishment." Adm. McHale paused to let the new president consider this.

"Personally, Ma'am, I'd consider it an honour to die for what I did," 'Pit Bull' added. *Hmmmm, I think he's serious,* Pillosi thought.

"Madame President, General Pruitt doesn't speak for all of us on that point," Air Force Gen. Saxon added quickly.

The other Joint Chiefs laughed. "But I believe he's saying that we understand if you have to bring charges against us. Our country was established on the rule of law. No one is above that law."

President Pillosi had heard enough. "Look, let's not discuss charges at this point. We have already charged President Trimp and Vice President Pens with treason and obstruction of justice regarding the Russian interference in our last election."

The elder stateswoman made sure to make eye contact with each member of the Joint Chiefs as she continued speaking. "The whole world is grateful that you had the foresight and courage to recognize three years ago that Donald Trimp was an impetuous, unhinged lunatic. I've discussed your case with our legal department. They believe that Trimp's 'order to launch' constituted an illegal order or 'unlawful command,' in military jargon. The only people 'howling' for your blood are the dangerous fanatics on Fox News who swore loyalty to Trimp in 2016." The Joint Chiefs seemed relieved to hear consoling words from their new commander. "The rest of the world is celebrating your actions as heroic, rather than treasonous."

"Gentlemen, our nation has been grievously wounded during Trimp's time as president," she continued steadfastly. "As leaders, we will need to work very hard to heal those wounds. So right now, we need good leaders more than ever. I hope I can count on your support going forward as we try our best to rebuild trust between the American people and her institutions."

"I've got two years left, Ma'am," "Pit Bull" Pruitt replied proudly. "And I'll give you everything I've got–all my effort, all my energy–in those two years."

The other Joint Chiefs had similar sentiments. As the military men were leaving and the new president's executive assistants were scrambling about in preparation for the next meeting, Nancy Pillosi had a final thought.

"General Pruitt?"

"Yes, Ma'am."

"If Trimp had launched all those missiles three days ago, what would have happened?" she asked, almost afraid of the answer.

"We wouldn't be having this discussion, Ma'am," the general replied grimly. "There's enough power in our nuclear arsenal to destroy the world 100 times over. The madman we recently called our president wanted to use it all to punish the Canadian prime minister over some Twitter insults."

Nancy Pillosi looked sad at hearing this news. *It's a reconfirmation of facts I already knew,* she thought.

"What in God's name were we thinking when we built up such an arsenal?" she asked. The question was directed at no one in particular, and everyone in the room, but mostly to herself.

"There is no simple answer to that question, Ma'am. But going forward, we need to consider how to reduce the power and influence of the military industrial complex," Gen. Pruitt answered, looking embarrassed.

"Ma'am, if it helps, we have a tremendous team of engineers that can help us safely disarm much of that destructive force," Gen. Saxon added.

Judging by the bustle in the room, it was clear the meeting was over. "Thank you, Gentlemen. I'd like to hear more about that very issue in the near future. A simple briefing note, perhaps?"

By way of response, the four Chiefs of Staff came smartly to attention, saluting their new commander in chief.

I'm not sure I'll ever get used to that, the new president thought to herself.

President Pillosi's new chief of staff cleared his throat. "Madame President, do you need a minute, or would you like to address the White House staff and the press? They are assembled in the foyer, as you requested."

"We've got a lot to do, Thomas. Let's press on," the 46th POTUS declared enthusiastically. "But I'm going let you lead the way, because I honestly don't know my way around here yet."

"It takes awhile, Ma'am. It's a big house."

The foyer was grander than President Pillosi recalled. Several hundred staff were assembled there: chefs, medics, clerks, tech support, mechanics, security personnel, drivers, butlers, gardeners and housekeepers. There were also 30-odd members of the Press Corps. For their part, the press looked astonished to be in the White House, and more astonished that the president had invited them.

"Ladies and Gentlemen, the President of the United States of America!" her chief of staff proclaimed loudly. Nancy Pillosi smiled and blushed simultaneously as the room erupted into cheering and applause. After a minute, the crowd began to settle down.

"I wanted to take a minute for us to get to know each other," the 46th POTUS began, walking towards the White House staff. "So, I'm Nancy," she said, extending her hand to the first chef in line, an older black man. "And you are?"

"Ma'am, I'm Justin Jackson," he replied, beaming with pride as he shook her hand.

"How long have you worked in the White House, Mr. Jackson?"

"Thirty-one years next month, Ma'am."

The new president spent the next 45 minutes meeting her staff, exchanging a few quick words with each of them. The Press Corps had a field day recording it.

"OK, don't quiz me later on all your names," she joked, returning to the centre of the room. "But I just wanted you to know that the American people appreciate the work that you've been doing here. Obviously, if you have been selected to work in the White House, you must be very good at what you do. So, I encourage you to be proud of yourselves, and the work that you do for our country. Please, give yourselves a well-deserved round of applause."

The president started it, and the staff themselves, blushing at the recognition, gradually picked it up.

"So now, just a few words to the Press Corps, if I may."

"Ma'am, we've been waiting for three years to be addressed by a president," a young lady from *The New York Times* replied, almost in tears but smiling.

President Pillosi smiled back good naturedly. "I know it hasn't been easy to be a journalist or reporter these past few years. It also hasn't been an easy time to be a left-leaning politician, if I'm being honest...*applause and relieved laughter*

"But nobody ever promised us easy. I can, however, promise you that I and our new administration will work hard to heal the division and mistrust that is hurting our country right now...*applause*

"And the best way to start to heal those wounds is by trusting each other again, by listening respectfully to each other's ideas, and working together to ensure that we make smart decisions..." *applause*

"So that's where we need to go," President Pillosi stated, switching to a more serious tone. "But I can't do this alone. It's a big job, and we're going to need a lot of people working together to get America back on track. And you members of the free press have a big role to play in this."

The room suddenly got much quieter.

"We are going to ask that you hold us, your government, accountable for our decisions. Question our decisions. Shine bright lights on the things you think may have been conceived in darkness. Because our freedom depends on a free press doing its job fairly, without discrimination or prejudice."

"What is a typical Canadian? Well, there's no such thing. Canada is one of the most cosmopolitan and multicultural countries in the world (Toronto and Vancouver are among the world's most cosmopolitan cities) and we are a nation of foreigners (except for our First Nations peoples) who often have little in common with one another. However, despite our diverse racial mix, Canada isn't a universal melting pot and has been called a cultural mosaic, where the country's multicultural approach emphasises the different backgrounds and cultures of its people. Canadians are one of the most difficult peoples to categorize and our country has been described as not so much a nation as a collection of different peoples on a continental scale. For a nation that's made up almost entirely of immigrants, it's hardly surprising that many Canadians have an identity crisis and spend a lot of time pondering 'The Great Canadian Question': 'What is a Canadian?'"

"A Canadian is someone who knows how to make love in a canoe."
–Pierre Berton, 1968

CHAPTER 3

Canadiana Special

Maple Ridge, British Columbia

Jill Burfitt's funeral was really more of a joyous celebration of a life well lived. She was well known and highly respected in Maple Ridge. The story of how Jill Burfitt had given her own life to save her daughter KT and her granddaughter Susanna was simultaneously heartwarming and heratbreaking. Her heroic role in stopping Susanna's abduction had been told around the world, but KT and Jill's friends had insisted that only people who knew Jill would be allowed to attend the service. Jill Burfitt had been a beloved teacher, avid golfer, girls' soccer player and coach, hockey player and coach, and curler. There were literally thousands of Jill and KT's friends who attended the service. Originally the plan was to have the service in the chapel of a local funeral home, but it quickly became apparent there wasn't enough room for those who wanted to attend. Five of Jill's closest friends had been instrumental in helping KT arrange the service to take place in the local arena. Considering they had just lost their mother/grandmother in very traumatic circumstances, KT and Susanna were holding up very well.

As a former journalist, KT knew how to tell a story. She spoke honestly and openly now at her mother's funeral. "Oh, my goodness. I can't thank you wonderful people enough for all the support you have given us these past few days." KT paused to sniffle and wipe away tears, which resulted in 2,200 people doing the same thing. She smiled. "But these really are tears of joy today. I honestly had forgotten how many friends my mother had. I'm absolutely thrilled that you took the time to be with us today. Now you may recall that my mom always enjoyed a good party."

KT paused while folks in the arena quietly murmured and laughed their assent. "You also know that if my mother were here today, she would tell you to raise a glass in memory of your friendship with her. So, I'd like you all to stay for a bit, so we can catch up and get re-acquainted. There's a free bar courtesy of, well, honestly, hundreds of people who donated money to support this service. And enough sandwiches and finger food to feed an army, thanks to our local churches who set this up, so please stay and help us eat all this."

She wiped some more tears, and again smiled through them. "I almost forgot, we have a book of memories up here that we'd love you to sign. Feel free to share any stories that you might have about your friendship with mom. And there is also an online condolence book that you can sign if you'd prefer. Ummmmm...I honestly don't know how to finish this. Thanks again for your incredible kindness to us. Please stick around if you can. We'd love to meet you. We love you, Mom," she said kissing two fingers and gently touching her mother's favourite picture. "And we love all of you amazing people," she finished, pointing to every corner of the packed arena.

KT stepped off the dais where her mother's ashes were displayed in a simple clay urn alongside treasured family photos. The crowd gradually erupted in polite applause as KT and Susanna walked towards the lounge at the back of the arena. The applause grew louder, so Susanna began to bow, blow kisses and curtsy to the crowd, which in turn made the crowd cheer and applaud even louder.

"Susanna, you are such a ham," KT teased, pulling the child closer and smiling.

"Mmmmmmmm, ham!" Susanna replied, laughing and rubbing her belly.

Ottawa, Ontario

Immediately after being elected, Elijah began to deliver on campaign promises. Change. The Independent People's Party had campaigned on change.

Elijah appointed Cabinet ministers from every political party, not just from the Independent members. This was done in order to hear all voices–Conservative, Liberal, Green, NDP and the Bloc Quebecois. It wasn't perfect. A caucus meeting among politicians with different ideologies, political beliefs and regional priorities was proving to be more challenging than the previous norm: a group of like-minded Conservatives or Liberals with a majority working together and voting along party lines. The new system worked. Not easily, but it worked. Polls indicated that the Canadian people felt like issues were actually being discussed from all viewpoints, rather than just being force-fed a Liberal or Conservative agenda as had happened for the first 150 years in Canadian politics.

Democracies all over the world were studying the Canadian government. Traditionally, the prime minister who won the election then appointed ministers from their own party to Cabinet positions. Nothing about Canada's new government was traditional.

The press had a field day as Elijah unveiled the new Cabinet. Like many things Elijah organized, the introduction of the Cabinet ministers was wildly entertaining and full of surprises. He was wearing a white tuxedo and matching top hat. The entire ensemble was festooned with red maple leaves.

"All right, let's get this party started!" Elijah had shouted enthusiastically. "Oh, and by the way, this is your Cabinet and your government. I'm expecting some good questions from our guests and the Press Gallery. Don't be shy. You have a question or comment, raise your hand. If you think anyone here is not a good fit for the portfolio we've selected, ask us. Let's talk it out!"

"He's more like a ringmaster at a freak show than a prime minister," whispered a crusty old journalist from the *Sun* to one of his peers.

"First, as minister of foreign affairs, the Honourable Dustin Trudel!" Elijah announced with a smile. The audience in Rideau Hall gasped, then applauded warmly as the former prime minister, and current leader of the Liberal Party in opposition, strode across the stage to shake Elijah's hand.

Multiple hands in the air from the press box.

"Prime Minister, why pick the leader of the opposition party to be in your Cabinet? It's highly unusual," asked the *Ottawa Citizen*.

"Well, Canada, standby for a whole bunch of highly unusual things from this government," Elijah responded. You could hear the audience inhale sharply. "We campaigned on different, we campaigned on change. Now, regarding Mr. Trudel as a minister in our Cabinet: Why wouldn't we want a former prime minister, who has excellent personal relations with most world leaders, as our minister of foreign affairs?"

"Mr. Trudel, how do you feel about your 'demotion' from prime minister to a Cabinet post?" asked the *Montreal Gazette*.

"Honestly, after each election, I'm always just thankful if I win my riding, and that I still have a job," Trudel responded good naturedly in French. *Laughter*

"I don't see the foreign affairs portfolio as a demotion. I see instead a very challenging job in a world that is rapidly changing. By including non-party members in the Cabinet, the prime minister is demonstrating that he wants to hear from all voices. It's a courageous and inspirational change from the status quo."

"How do your wife and your family feel now that you are no longer the prime minister, Mr. Trudel?" a young lady in the audience asked.

"I've been married for some years now, so I'm pretty well trained." *More laughter*

"When people ask me how my wife feels about something, I've learned it's better to let her respond," Trudel gestured to his wife. *Louder laughter and applause*

Sophia stood up smiling in the audience. "How do I feel?" She paused for a moment. "Relieved." The audience applauded and laughed. "Being prime minister is a time-consuming job," she continued. "Maybe now Dustin can spend more time with us." *Applause*

Elijah continued his introductions. "Danni Grey Eyes, the former chief of the Mistawasis First Nation in Saskatchewan, is minister for aboriginal affairs. *Applause*

"Ladies and Gentlemen, your minister of education, Benjamin Big Canoe." A*pplause, wolf whistles from a few of the braver women in the audience*

Benjamin had been on the cover on tabloids worldwide the day after the election. The photo showed a lean, chiselled and ridiculously handsome Benjamin Big Canoe wearing buckskin pants and a vest. *HOT AND SMART* the headline shouted. *MEET CANADA'S NEW MP's.*

"Is it true that you and the minister of aboriginal affairs are an item?" a young MTV reporter shouted.

"It sure is, and I think I'm very lucky to have such a wonderful girlfriend." A*www*

"That's not gonna be a problem, is it?" Danni Grey Eyes interjected, teasing the audience. *Nooooo,* the audience shouted.

"Minister Big Canoe, is it true you were a professional hockey player?" a reporter wondered.

"I knew there'd be a hockey question at an introduction of Canadian Cabinet ministers," Benjamin joked. *Laughter*

"But no, that was my dad. I'll tell him you remember him though…" *More laughter*

"I'm just a boring old political science professor." *More laughter and applause*

"Harjit Singh is a former Army commander who has served Canada with honour and distinction, both here at home, and while deployed in Afghanistan and Bosnia," Elijah continued. "He retains his portfolio as minister of defence. *Applause*

"No questions for our minister of defence?" Elijah wondered aloud. "Ah, yes. Mr. Sinclair."

"Mr. Singh, you've held this portfolio for several years now. Can you comment on the woeful state of today's Armed Forces?" the curmudgeon from the *Sun* was wondering. "Our military is now smaller in numbers of troops than it was in 1938. In 1945, Canada had the third-largest navy and fourth-largest army in the world, and our sailors, soldiers and air force personnel were highly regarded worldwide. However, since 1945, our military has been reduced to a mere shadow of its former glory. In 1945, we had 1.1 million Canadians in uniform. Today there are less than 100,000 military personnel in the Canadian Forces. In light of the recent attempted attack on our sovereignty by the US, does this government have a plan to strengthen our military?"

"It's true that our military has declined sharply since World War Two," the defence minister began. "As you correctly stated, we have shrunk to less than 100,000 personnel, from an all-time high of 1.1 million personnel at the end of World War Two."

The minister looked briefly at Elijah, who nodded and smiled. "It's interesting that you mention 1938," the defence minister continued. "At that time, Canada and much of the world were locked in a great depression, somewhat similar to the economic situation we are seeing today. Most economists and historians agree that World War Two ended the Great Depression by employing millions of troops and manufacturing weapons of war." Hajit Singh fell silent for a moment, but he clearly wasn't finished speaking, as he moved closer to the audience in Rideau Hall.

"After the Second World War, Canadians didn't put defence spending or maintenance of our Armed Forces as a high priority. So, like anything that is not attended to, our military withered and atrophied to the point it is at today…"

"Minister, we can all agree that our military is in deplorable condition," the curmudgeon interjected abruptly. "But my question was: What is your government's plan to fix it?"

Harjit Singh looked again at Elijah, eyebrows raised.

"Go ahead, Harjit," the new prime minister smiled and encouraged his minister of defence.

"We intend to pass legislation for all Canadians under 25 years of age to be conscripted in our military or other suitable government departments for a period of 18 months," Harjit Singh bluntly told the crowd at Rideau Hall, and the millions watching at home.

The crowd at Rideau Hall was shocked and stunned into momentary silence. Then the Press Gallery erupted, every arm was raised, every voice shouting.

The former outrageous talk show host and now new prime minister stepped forward to join Harjit Singh at the front of the stage. He raised his arms, palms up, asking for silence. When the crowd had subsided to a noise resembling a buzzing beehive, he spoke quietly.

"See, I told you this government was gonna be different," Elijah began. "We can't keep doing the same things we have been doing for the past 50 years and expect different results." He began to pace the stage, engaging the audience, speaking to all of them, plus all the folks in TV land.

"Listen, don't get all freaked out about this conscription thing. Mr. Sinclair asked a fair question. Fixing our military and simultaneously investing in Canada's future will be one of our first priorities. We just got elected last week, so this issue is still very much in the planning stages. But here is what we know so far. We know that we can invest in today's youth and give them some tremendous opportunity. We are going to ensure that your period of mandatory service will be safe and enjoyable. You will be paid a fair wage."

Every arm was still raised in the Press Gallery, and the journalists were beginning to make more noise. Elijah smiled at them and the audience. "I know you have a lot more questions on this topic. Please, hold those questions for another hour or so. Let me introduce the rest of the Cabinet, and then we'll answer all your questions. I promise."

The noise in the gallery resided slowly.

"Elizabeth Day has been a heroic environmental champion and crusader for many years," Elijah stated, continuing with Cabinet introductions like he hadn't just dropped a conscription bombshell. "She is the leader of the Green Party and was obviously born to be the environment minister." *Applause*

"Ms. Day, were you surprised when the prime minister asked you to be minister of the environment?" CTV News wondered.

"Well, yes and, no, of course not." *Laughter*

"It's unheard of for a prime minister to appoint Cabinet members from outside their own party, hence my surprise. But as the leader of the Green Party, I've made environmental protection my life's work. I've spent six months in jail protesting various corporations that put profit before our planet." *Applause*

"Folks, there is no Planet B. If we destroy this one for money, that is a tragedy. As your minister of the environment, it's my job to make sure that we protect the natural world from those persons who would exploit our resources for profit. Not gonna happen on my watch," she warned, wagging a finger at the television cameras." *Applause*

Less Izmore's story was quite well known. The 65-year-old hippie and former bank executive (in the 1980s) had more recently been the elder of a commune in British Colombia known as SimpleTown. He was now the minister of finance of a G7 nation. Elijah simply introduced him as "a man of tremendous intellect, insight and experience."

"Mr. Izmore, when were you last employed in the finance sector?" a reporter from the *Vancouver Sun* queried.

"1986," Less answered.

"Mr. Prime Minister, is there no one with more recent financial sector experience that might make a better finance minister than Mr. Izmore?" the *Sun* reporter continued.

"No," Elijah replied. "But if he sucks at this, we'll find someone better." All the ministers smiled. Elijah's open honesty was both refreshing and frightening all at once. Refreshing to those persons who enjoyed open honest answers. Frightening to those persons who didn't like change.

"Give me a chance," Less added amiably. "The finance sector hasn't changed in hundreds of years. It's actually quite simple. No person, or family, or corporation or government should repeatedly spend more than they can expect to be able to repay. If you don't like the direction we are headed in after a few months, tell Elijah to fire me. I think you'll find he's a great listener." *Applause*

"Charley, c'mon out!" Elijah shouted. The audience stood and cheered.

Charley Shackleton, a simple 72-year-old farmer from Elgin County, Ontario, was minister of agriculture. He had often appeared on Elijah's talk show. He was normally accompanied by his loyal farm dog, Fred. Charley always wore a ball cap, striped coveralls and boots, and had a faded red handkerchief in his pocket. Today was no different.

"Charley, are we ever going to see you in a suit?" a reporter shouted.

"Well, I s'ppose I'll wear one at my funeral," Charley responded. *Laughter and applause*

"But what I'm wearin' now is my business suit," he continued in that down-home style that people loved. "I've always been a farmer, and I'm proud of that." *Applause*

"So, if I'm gonna be the minister of agriculture, I want all our farmers to know that we can talk in simple terms. I never did no agriculturin' in a suit." Charley waved. Fred barked. The audience applauded.

"Full disclosure, Canada," Elijah said. "This next young lady is the love of my life…" *Crazy foot-stomping, hand-clapping applause*

"But that is not why I selected Juliette Sparks as our minister of youth." The audience went quiet as Elijah paused, and Juliette came onto the stage and stood by her fellow ministers.

Juliette Sparks, 23, was the president of the student union in Saint Mary's University in Halifax. Then she won her riding of Halifax Citadel, and became the youngest Cabinet minister in Canadian history.

"I selected Juliette as our minister of youth because she is a rare talent—a unifier, a dream chaser, an overachiever, a champion of the downtrodden, and quite frankly, an inspirational person." Elijah was moving again, pulling the crowd in. "So please, give her a chance to impress you. Give all of us a chance. We are new at this. I can promise you some simple things. We will work hard. We will be open and honest with you. And we aren't afraid to explore new ideas."

Elijah and his Cabinet ministers took a bow. The question period following the Cabinet introduction lasted five hours.

The first legislation the IPP passed was a bill that lowered the pay and pension plan for federal politicians by 25 per cent. To say that was popular would be an understatement—several other countries had since followed suit. Nobody seemed to think it was a bad idea to pay politicians less money.

The next legislation passed was the Food Additive Tax also known as the "FAT Tax." In a nutshell, the FAT doubled the cost of unhealthy "junk" foods like pop, chips, Pizza Pops and similar snacks. Some of the revenue generated from this tax was used to lower the cost of locally produced "real" food: vegetables, fruits, dairy, grains, legumes, meats, fish, etc. The remainder of the revenue was used to supplement health care costs. The FAT was unpopular at first– obviously with people who like junk food–but most folks had quit whining about it. The minister of health had summed it up nicely. "You can still have unhealthy food, but the extra money you pay for it is going to help us cover your medical costs if it's a regular habit."

There were some additional benefits. The medical community was already seeing a reduction in obesity-related illnesses, especially among youth. Within a few months, the cost of feeding a family had lowered by 20 to 30 per cent. With unhealthy food now much more expensive, essentially everyone but the richest people had to buy the more affordable real food items. From a sociological perspective, many families also reported that having to prepare meals from scratch had become a fun family activity. Also, the tax revenue enabled agricultural subsidization. This increased the number of Canadian farmers significantly, and new farms (or former farms that had gone fallow) were starting or being reborn on a daily basis in every region. The backyard gardens popular 50 or 60 years ago were also back in vogue.

"The FAT Tax is a win, win, win, win, win," the health minister stated proudly. "Canadians are eating healthier foods, it has increased agricultural employment and output, it's bringing families back to the kitchen table, and it's lowered the cost of buying food."

After the FAT, the government passed a bill which significantly taxed carbon. This was easily the most-hated piece of legislation the new government proposed and passed.

"The rationale and contents of our carbon tax bill are multipronged," explained the ministers in rowdy Town Halls across the country. The eight Cabinet ministers involved put in a couple of tough months selling this to Canadians, some of whom felt: "It's my God-given right to drive my truck."

Less Izmore and Elizabeth Day generally co-hosted the Town Halls, with moral support from other ministers. "First, we want to thank you for coming to this Town Hall meeting," Less began. "The bill contains input from the ministries of environment, finance, revenue, natural resources, trade, research and development, agriculture, fisheries and oceans, and transport."

"We intend to lower our dependence on fossil fuels and reduce our carbon footprint so that our children can inherit a healthy planet," Elizabeth Day continued. "So, the tax directly on purchases of fuels for vehicles will encourage Canadians to consider other options: carpool, take a bus, ride a bike, walk. It's not sustainable to think that every adult Canadian needs to own a car or cars and drive everywhere by themselves. The tax revenue from these fuel sales will be used to subsidize the cost of public transport where possible, and to fund research and development into renewable energy sources."

The carbon tax also had massive trade implications that weren't exactly embraced by many Canadians. In fact, a lot of people hated the idea. "Items purchased from outside Canada will be subject to a 20 per cent carbon tax," the trade minister explained to jeering crowds from

BC to Newfoundland. "These items have been brought to our country by ships, or planes, or trains, or trucks that are burning fuel and hurting our planet. We are going to tax those imported items and use the revenue to subsidize Canadian businesses that produces the products we currently import."

The environment minister often added: "And those items being produced in Canada will need to travel less distance, so again, it's a win-win. The planet gets to heal as less fuel is burned, and more Canadians will be working: making and growing the items we consume."

"The carbon tax also has a production element," Less Izmore Less explained in Vancouver at the first rally.

"It's a F@#% ing Simpleton policy," shouted an angry middle-aged man. "And you F@#%ing dope-smoking Simpletons are ruining this country!" The crowd was cheering him on, so he vented for a few minutes more. Less waited patiently for him to run out of steam.

"Sir, indeed it is a Simpleton policy. And I'm proud to be called a Simpleton, because I come from a community called Simpletown, where we live our lives in a simple way." Less finally responded quietly when the man finished his rant. "Now let me tell you why. There are economical, environmental and sociological benefits of producing or growing goods by hand or real horsepower in Canada, rather than having those goods imported or mass produced in factories overseas or here at home."

Less stepped out from behind the podium and moved to the front of the stage. He was an engaging speaker who made each member of the audience feel as if their hippie grandfather were speaking directly to them.

"Look, the Simpleton policy will give more Canadians meaningful jobs. People with meaningful jobs have money to spend in our economy and they feel good that the work they do has value and contributes to a healthy society." Less kept talking as he moved across the stage from left to right.

The environment minister jumped in to help Less. "By making more things locally and growing more of our food here, we reduce the need to ship things in from other parts of the world, which reduces carbon use and slows climate change," Elizabeth Day said. "So now do you see the benefits of the Simpleton policy?"

As the Town Halls (and accompanying media) explaining the new policies worked their way east across the country, they eventually met with less hostile resistance. The public were beginning to buy in to the logic of the plan.

Canada's new government had also pulled the plug on NAFTA early into their mandate. "It's just not working for us, folks," Charley Shackleton often explained to the crowd in his homespun manner. "We can make and grow everything we need right here and put a whole buncha Canadians back to work."

Many of the IPP's achievements were considered significant from the viewpoint of anyone concerned with sustainability, environmental protection, and narrowing the gap between the uber rich and uber poor. However, most people around the world (except hard-core Trimpanzees) agreed that one of the Canadian government's more significant acts had driven Donald Trimp out of the White House and into an asylum early in 2020.

History tells us that Trimp reached "peak crazy" when Canada's controversial and independent Prime Minister Elijah delivered a televised ultimatum to President Donald J. Trimp.

"Canada and the United States have been good neighbours for a long time now. However, Canada can no longer sit idly by while the Trimp Administration continues its criminal environmental assault on our planet. Much of the environmental damage that has occurred recently is directly affecting Canada and Canadians negatively, due to our geographical proximity with the US. This tragedy is not limited to North America. The Trimp Administration's environmental policy—or lack thereof—is now regarded as the largest threat to our planet today.

"Mr. Trimp, the damage you are doing in your greedy quest for dirty fuel and dirtier money is endangering our whole planet, not just your own people. Therefore, the Government of Canada has no choice but to issue your administration an ultimatum. We demand that the USA return to global environmental summit meetings and commit in good faith to international target agreements regarding carbon reduction. We further demand that the USA put back in place the Environmental Protection Agency, with the authority and acts that existed in 2016 prior to the Trimp Administration's assault on our global environment."

Donald J. Trimp did not receive ultimatums, he gave them. Elijah's ultimatum was the final straw. Trimp had never been mentally stable (despite his own famous tweets to the contrary.) Thanks to the magic of social media, President Trimp had been lambasted with more insults than anyone on the planet, ever, in the history of ever. Now please don't start feeling sorry for Donald Trimp. He deserved every one of these insults, plus many more. Just go back and (re) read *The Mouse Who Poked an Elephant* if you need more insight into what a hideous and horrible human being Donald Trimp was, and why he tried to nuke Canada.

Elijah was Donald Trimp's worst enemy and adversary. Trimp hated Elijah even more than he hated Mallory Clifton or Barrack Oobima. Elijah was everything Trimp hated rolled up into human form. Smart. Funny. Black. Sexy. Handsome. Black. Trilingual. Well-spoken. Black. Admired. Beloved. Honest. Black. Resolute. Defiant. Tough. Black.

Elijah looked like the love child of Lanny Kravits and Bayonce. Elijah went by just one name, like Cher and Jesus. Elijah had a big black Afro, and a super hot black girlfriend called Juliette with an equally large Afro. Together they looked like the sexiest, hottest, smartest people on the planet. Elijah was a child soldier who had escaped Somalia and was raised by lesbians in Vancouver. He had turned down a Rhodes Scholarship. Before he became Canada's prime minister, Elijah hosted Canada's most-popular TV show, *Power to the People*, which lampooned and ridiculed men like Trimp.

First and foremost though, Donald Trimp hated Elijah because of Melanie. Melanie Trimp was a notoriously beautiful but very unhappy woman. During her marriage to "The Donald," her face was a constant mask of pain and sadness. In every photo of her looking at Donald Trimp, people imagined the cartoon bubble caption from Melanie was: "You were supposed to be dead by now." Melanie only ever smiled and looked capable of love at the sight of or at the thought of one person: Elijah.

Trimp, deep in his black heart, knew that Melanie lusted after Elijah. His deepest, darkest nightmare was that Melanie wanted to "make boom-boom" with Elijah. That nightmare always made him lurch awake in a cold sweat at 3 a.m. *Prime tweetin' time....*

Trimp was the most despised man on the planet in 2020. Elijah was the Anti-Trimp. Almost everyone on the planet (minus Trimp and the Trimpanzees) loved Elijah and Canada's new no-nonsense Independent government.

So, on January 21, 2020, Trimp called Elijah's bluff, rejected Elijah's ultimatum, and threatened to invade and annex Canada.

Elijah responded by cutting off electricity, oil and natural gas to the USA, plunging approximately 60 million Americans into cold darkness.

Americans responded by fleeing to Canada (at Elijah's invitation) or by rioting in the streets.

Trimp responded to this by attempting to launch the USA's entire nuclear arsenal at Canada.

"Listen, I really can't take credit for driving Donald Trimp crazy," Elijah stated in an interview with *The Washington Post*. "I mean, c'mon, that wasn't even a long drive. Everything happens for a reason. I believe Mr.

Trimp's purpose on this stage was to encourage people to get involved in politics and to teach us how not to behave. So, yeah, mission accomplished." Elijah paused to give two thumbs up, which ended up being the cover photo for that day's paper and a weekly magazine. "Now looking to the future, I'm confident that the American people will enjoy some vigorous political debate in the run-up to the election scheduled for November the fourth."

"Elijah, do you have a favourite candidate?"

"No, I do not. And I'm not an American citizen, so it wouldn't matter if I did."

"Are you concerned that the American system of governance is a duopoly?"

"Oh, I see now you are just trying to get me in trouble," Elijah smiled. "Look, here is what we told the Canadian people two years ago when we started the Independent People's Party. If you consistently elect Liberals to fix a Conservative mess, and then elect Conservatives to fix a Liberal mess, and then repeat that cycle for 150 or 250 years, your system might be a little stagnant."

"Do you believe the United States is ready for a shake-up to the current political status quo?"

"Again, it's not my country, so it doesn't matter what I think. But the timing certainly seems right to try something different."

The Independent People's Party believed that professional politicians who served unlimited multiple terms made decisions based on things that would get them, and their party re-elected, rather than what might be best for their constituents or the country. The idea of restricting the duration of an individual's political service was being discussed and considered in multiple democracies such as Norway, Denmark, New Zealand and Sweden.

Elijah's Cabinet was an eclectic group, formed and led by an eccentric person. The discussion was often heated, intense and passionate, but Elijah insisted that "at every Cabinet meeting we will be discussing one or two main topics. I want the start of every Cabinet meeting to be like a brain-storming session. There is no topic or idea that is off limits. Don't you dare remain silent in these meetings because you think your input or idea regarding that topic is different from what the group thinks or that it's crazy. We need different and crazy."

One of Elijah's election promises had been to legislate a maximum four-year period of service for elected politicians. This was proving to be difficult, as the Canadian Constitution would need significant amendments in order to pass the bill.

"Brother, trust Dustin and I on this one. You do not wanna open up the can of whoop-ass that is the Canadian Constitution," Benjamin Big Canoe told him. "I studied constitutional law. It is not easy, or pretty, or fun."

Dustin Trudel, nodded in vigorous agreement. "Elijah, Ben's right. The Constitution is a Pandora's box that you don't want to look into. The legal steps required to change even a comma are immense. Every politician who has tried to change the Constitution has wished they hadn't."

"Every politician who wanted to be re-elected, you mean?" Elijah responded angrily. "The whole reason for putting a four-year cap on service was to enable elected officials to make smart, courageous decisions without worrying about their possible re-election."

"But if the legislation is going to be painfully, horribly, impossibly difficult, let's not tackle it," Danni Grey Eyes suggested to Elijah. "It's not a battle we need to fight. Let's save our strength. You're a great communicator. Just explain to Canadians that this change isn't possible through legislation. If you believe that a politician should only serve four years, then you, and I, and every other politician can choose not to run again on principle."

"Son, it's like my Uncle Fred used to tell me," Charley interjected. *"God grant me the serenity to accept the things I cannot change, the courage to change the things I can, and the wisdom to know the difference"* Charley stated seriously, with a grandfatherly hand on Elijah's shoulder.

"Your Uncle Fred used to quote Reinhold Niebuhr? The same Uncle Fred who got hit by lightning twice? The same Uncle Fred you named your last five dogs after?" Elijah asked.

Charley looked surprised that Elijah remembered the legacy of Uncle Fred. "Yep, that's him. Well, he never said it after the second lightning strike, of course." Charley said quietly.

You can't just ignore a line like that. It was one of those statements you had to follow up on.

"The lightning strike killed him?" Elijah asked, almost dreading the answer.

"Oh, heaven's, no. Uncle Fred lived another 20 years after that second strike. It left him deaf and dumb."

"Ahhhh, that's awful," Juliette chimed in.

Charley looked thoughtful. "Well, it wasn't all bad. His wife Martha used to nag him constantly about drinkin' moonshine in the barn and not goin' to church and cheatin' at cards. So, on the upside, as you kids like to say, he didn't hafta hear that anymore."

It usually took a minute for the group to regain its composure after Charley shared some down-home wisdom with them.

Elijah wiped his eyes with a Kleenex and checked his watch. "All righty then, thanks for this. Let's go do parliamenty stuff."

Democracy Dies in Darkness
—*Masthead of* The Washington Post,
adopted Feb. 27, 2017

CHAPTER 4

Yay, Daddy's Home!

Washington DC

"Welcome to the first rally of the Independent People's Party of America!" Senator Barney Saunders boomed in his clipped Yankee accent to a crowd of 1.7 million persons. It was the biggest crowd ever assembled on the National Mall.

Roar...The crowd went crazy.

"Welcome to a new day." *Roar...* People 10 miles away from the Mall reported the crowd noise sounded like a giant angry beast coming out of hibernation. Others described the sound as more like hundreds of rockets or jet planes taking off all at once.

Most Americans were simply euphoric that Trimp was no longer president. Hope for a new future and a new start just seemed to be the icing on the cake, the cherry on the sundae.

The senior senator from Vermont continued. "I want to introduce you to the next president of the United States..." Barney was interrupted by an ear-splitting, ground-shaking roar that you could feel in your bones.

"From the great State of Illinois…representing the people of America…Michelle Oobima!" Barney Saunders shouted into the delirium that was the National Mall.

Michelle, Barrack and their two daughters came onto the stage all holding hands to deafening roars. After several minutes, the crowd calmed down.

"It's so nice to see all of you here today," Michelle announced pleasantly. More pandemonium. She held her hands up asking for quiet. It took a minute. Large screens all along the Mall were blinking "QUIET, PLEASE."

"OK. Let's take turns. You let me speak for a minute, and then we'll make some noise. Sound good?" The crowd rooooooooooaaaaaared its approval. When it finally died down, Michelle continued.

She spoke quietly, but the sound system carried her voice clearly over largest crowd ever assembled at the Mall. The big screens showed a confident and determined-looking former FLOTUS.

"Let's not look backwards," she said, holding up her hands to a crowd that seemed ready to explode.

"Let's not worry about last week, or last year. Let's move forward.

"Let's start to rebuild and heal America. We, the people, got this. And today, truly, is the first day of the rest of our lives." The crowd took it away for another minute or two.

"So, I want to start by introducing my running mate…" The crowd couldn't be held back this time. An insane roar shook leaves on trees, sound that pulsed in sonic waves crashed over Washington DC.

"Well, it was supposed to be a surprise," Michelle Oobima said, smiling once the storm died down. "But it seems like you know who's coming out…" She gave the crowd another minute, but the sound didn't die down any. Michelle's husband whispered in her ear. Eventually the noise subsided.

"Ladies and Gentlemen, I give you, the next vice president of the United States…Dwain John- Stone!"

Dwain John-Stone. Yes. The former wrestler turned actor, also known simply as "The Stone."

The Stone was aka "The People's Champion" and "the most electrifying figure in sports entertainment." The winner of *People* magazine's "Sexiest Man Alive" strode through the curtains at the back of the stage and warmly greeted the Oobimas.

Ornithologists and birdwatchers in the capital region noted that the noise at the IPP rally was so loud that no birds were sighted within a 12-mile radius of the Mall.

The rally lasted another three hours. The list of Independent candidates running for elected office was impressive.

Seven highly regarded Democrat senators, 19 Democrat representatives and five Democrat governors were running as Independents.

Hermann Schultz, Starbucks CEO, was stepping away from the coffee business to run as a representative in Washington.

Three incumbent Republican senators, seven House representatives and two governors were leaving the Republican party to run as Independent politicians.

Jesus "The Body" Ventura—former Minnesota governor, professional wrestler and Navy SEAL––was making a strong case as representative for his home district in Minnesota.

The former "governator" and Mr. Olympia, actor Arnold Schwarzenegro, was offering his services as a representative in California.

The Independents had also attracted a who's who list of media personalities: John Olivero, Sarah Silverstein, Trevor Noa and Chelsea Chandler were running as Independent representative candidates.

Abdul Kareem Jabar, Karley Lloyd, Joe Mantano, Christy Yamaguchi and Cal Ropken Jr had always been competitive sports heroes. Now they were bringing some serious intensity and star power to the political arena as Independent candidates.

Most (but not all) of the Independent candidates were on the younger side compared to their opponents in the two traditional parties. Most (but not all) were well educated. Compared to the two traditional parties, the Independent Party was fielding many more visible minority candidates, many more female candidates and very few candidates who were born with a silver spoon.

When the Independents began meeting in 2017, they realized that there were multiple reasons why an Independent politician had never run. Throughout American history, the two traditional parties secretly colluded to ensure that the American people only had two choices: essentially a duopoly. Neither the Democratic nor Republican party ever, ever, ever wanted a third challenger. Both parties were fully aware that their future hope of political power was in making sure that people could only choose between left or right. Savvy Democrat and

Republican party leaders both understood that it was OK for the other party to rule now and then. "The pendulum of public opinion will swing back our way in four or eight years…"

The first and biggest obstacle to breaking a duopoly? Money. Normally, a political party with a large reserve of money could attract the best candidates, because they could spend massive amounts of money advertising for that candidate (or attacking the opposition's candidate). In 2020 a donor could give $834,000 in donations to one of the two traditional parties annually, but only $2,700 to any other party. So, for the past number of years, the Republican and Democratic parties won seats in both the Senate and the House of Representatives by outspending their opponents.

But it was no secret that money donated to political parties also normally had strings attached. As average citizens became more aware of who donated what in their riding, "following the money" wasn't all that difficult.

Imagine that a large mining corporation or family wanted to operate a pit mine for coal, but some pesky environmental protection laws forbade open-pit mining in that region. The corporation or family then donates big money to a party willing to change that law. That same party can spend money on spin doctors who tell people how good the mining jobs will be for that area, new schools will be built, *"our young people won't have to move away,"* the corporation will make sure they won't damage the environment, and so forth.

The people in that region may eventually begin to believe that open-pit mining will be a good thing for their region, and they elect the politician who has been fighting for their jobs. At the same time, those people opposed to open-pit mining could be tarred with any number of unsavory brushes: "hippie, communist, tree-hugger, elitist...*mining's too dirty for you, college boy?*"

So, for the past 100 years or so, money talked. Money bought politicians, and those politicians were obliged to do the bidding of their wealthy donors.

"Now Jim, Pappy and I have been big donors over these past years. What we'd really like to see is: environmental laws relaxed, female wages held lower than males, minimum wages held low, minority persons denied the vote, corporate tax reduced, segregated schools, protected parkland given a green light for fracking, approval for this stadium/golf course/casino/pit mine on donated municipal property..."

You can almost smell the bourbon in the room, can't you? Jest a couple good ole boys takin' care of business.

Joe Baden was polling in the lead for the Democratic Party, with Jim Kennedy and Andre Cuomo hot on his heels, followed by six or seven other reasonably good (but not very well-known) candidates. As is normal in US primaries, the nominees were busy tearing each other apart in order to run as president. Some of "Uncle Joe's" past indiscretions as Oobima's VP were being uncovered, but it wasn't anything sensational on a Trimpian level. Joe was likeable enough, he seemed like an upgrade from Mr.

Trimp, (but didn't almost everyone?) and he had some significant experience in the trenches.

Jim Kennedy was very popular with anyone leaning left, and he was a good motivational speaker, but he had little political experience. Some Americans were understandably nervous about electing yet another trust-fund millionaire president.

Andre Cuomo was the current governor of New York, whose father Marco had also been a governor, so there were a couple of generations of skeleton-filled closets coming to light there.

Some Democrat senators previously believed to be potential contenders to the throne a few years ago—Kamala Morris, Kristin Gillislee and Elizabeth Worrin, to name a few—had recently announced that they would be seeking re-election as Independents when their terms were up.

The Republican primary had even less reason for hope. Mikki Haley, Trimp's hard-hittin' UN ambassador, was winning a lot of right-wing hearts with her tough talk.

But the "tough girl" vote among the Grand Old Party faithful was being split between Haley and infamous Alaskan insaniac "the drilla from Wasilla," aka: "Governor Mooselini," aka Sarah Palon. Scared yet?

Wait—it gets more frightening—because polluting an already murky swamp even further was Steve Bannin, who appealed to those on the very furthest lunatic right fringe of a right-wing party.

Those feeling nostalgic for times when Republicans weren't viewed as dangerously nationalistic nutbars could consider Todd Cruz, Marco Rubion or Jeb Busch. The problem was Republicans had been beaten over the head with the nationalistic racist stick for so long, it was getting difficult to attract new blood. Plus, like the Democrats, several of their best-known and most-respected moderate Republican senators and representatives sitting in their respective houses were running for re-election as Independents.

A 2016 poll of American voters taken one month before the 2016 election indicated that 78 per cent of Americans would have voted for an Independent president rather than cast a vote for Donald Trimp or Mallory Clifton. A similar Gallup Poll in April of 2016 indicated that 44 per cent of Americans identified as Independent (a party that didn't exist), with 31 per cent identifying as Democrats and 25 per cent as Republican. Both established parties and the individuals representing those parties were viewed as being too corrupt, too beholden to their corporate donors, and willing to do or say anything to stay in power.

> *"Democrat or Republican? What's the difference? There is no difference. Can you smell what these crooks are cookin'? They are generally just smooth-talking criminals who sold their souls to their corporate overlords."–Dwain John-Stone, 2016.*

On the sixth day of her new job as POTUS, former House speaker Nancy Pillosi was meeting in the White House with members of her new Cabinet when a very odd thing happened.

The 46th POTUS was interrupted by the rather abrupt entrance of 20 heavily armed members of Team America in their trademark black riot gear.

"Nancy Pillosi," stated the senior officer, "you are under arrest."

"I'm the president of the United States," sputtered an obviously shocked and angry Pillosi.

"Wrong, Nancy," said Donald J. Trimp, walking quickly into the room.

"I'm the real president," he sneered. "Remember when I told you years ago that I never, ever lose?"

Nancy Pillosi still looked pretty surprised and angry. She started to speak, but Trimp backhanded her hard across the face, with a surprisingly small hand for such a large man.

"It's a rhetorical question, Nancy. That means there is no answer required."

"What about the rest of these people, Daddy?" Ivanka Trimp asked. Her father surveyed the room with an appraising eye.

"Pumpkin, let's have a Cabinet meeting with both the former and more recent advisors. We can pick the best people for each job."

"You mean just like you used to do on *The Apprentice*?"

"Exactly, honey," Donald said to Ivanka, smiling. "Isn't she terrific?" he said to his minions, who quickly agreed.

Vice President Mike Pens entered the room like a wooden puppet. "All secure, Sir. The White House is yours again."

"Great job, Mike. Just the best," Trimp replied cheerfully. "Hey, isn't it great to be back in the saddle again?" Donald Trimp asked his second in command, playfully punching him in the shoulder.

"It sure is, Mr. President," Pens relied robotically.

"Daddy, can I be secretary of state?" Ivanka gushed while hugging her father.

"Sure, honey. Anything you want."

"So, if Canada is not a people, not a nation, possibly not even a nation state, what are we? I would argue we are merely a collection of people who happen to be moving in roughly the same direction. Occasionally we have a leader who marshals us together, to walk in one particular direction, or to march to a specific rhythm. But only occasionally, and never for long. No, we remain the same colour on the map not because of a strong sense of shared identity or a common purpose, but because we simply haven't had much of a reason to split up. Yet."
—Scott Gilmore, April 2018

CHAPTER 5

Jets or Bush Planes?

Ottawa, Ontario

The Independent People's Party was rapidly expanding Canada's Armed Forces and putting a lot of people back to work. Nearly 900,000 young Canadians had been drafted for a one-year period of mandatory service in the militia or naval reserve since the IPP had won the election. Following the one-year period of service, reserve personnel returned to their units two weeks each year to upgrade training.

The basic training for personnel was a four-week course run at local armories and reserve units. The new recruits were trained in: drill, deportment and discipline, first aid, outdoor survival, and firefighting. Those personnel who were willing were also given small-arms training on rifles and pistols.

After the completion of their basic training, militia personnel normally worked on civic and municipal projects. Military personnel were embedded in multiple municipal, provincial and federal government departments: maintaining public spaces, working as labourers on publicly funded construction projects, landscaping, snow shovelling, painting, fixing roads, picking up roadside litter, maintaining arenas and pools, visiting and caring for seniors in retirement facilities, and helping farmers plant and harvest crops were a few examples of possible employment for militia members.

All Canadian militia personnel were trained primarily for emergency events: firefighting, crowd control, aid to civil power, disaster relief in the event of floods, hurricanes, tornadoes, earthquakes.

The Canadian Disaster Assistance Response Team (DART) was made up of volunteer militia soldiers, sailors and air force personnel willing to deploy. DART was multiplying rapidly, exponentially. On its formation in 1996, the team consisted of 200 personnel. With the massive recent expansion of the militia, DART now had 4,600 members. They were a highly trained group of personnel capable of providing assistance anywhere in the world on short notice.

"No matter where in the world we deploy as DART members, we always hear two wonderful things," DART's commanding officer was proud of explaining. Col. Marie Pierre-Paul emigrated to Canada from Haiti as a four-year-old girl. "First, we hear how glad people are that we are there to help in a time of urgent need. Second, we never get tired of hearing people tell us how impressed people are with the helpful spirit of our troops. So, yes, I'm incredibly proud to command a team whose basic mission is to restore hope in regions where natural disasters or war have caused human suffering."

The Canadian government had been trying to acquire new jets to replace its antiquated fleet of CF-18s for some years. It was the topic at that morning's caucus meeting.

"Why jets?" Danni Grey Eyes asked the minister of defence. "Jets are stupidly expensive and only good for warfighting. We can build 15,000 bush planes right here in Canada for less money than 50 jets."

Before Harjit Singh could respond, Finance Minister Less Izmore added his thoughts. "Harjit, Danni is right. Jets have a limited role—to kill other jets or drop bombs on people. They serve no other useful purpose. But imagine a massive fleet of bush planes flown by our militia pilots. They would help us open up the North again. We could connect and supply First Nation communities better than we are currently doing. Bush planes can do coastal surveillance for illegal shipping and invasions of our sovereignty. They can do fisheries patrols cheaply, they can deliver supplies and personnel to work camps, they can do search and rescue, they can help fight wildfires. Harjit, bush planes opened up the North, and then we sort of forgot about them, and the people who live up there."

"Yes, I understand your points," Harjit Singh responded thoughtfully. "But I am the minister of defence, so my first priority is to find planes that will be useful in defending our nation should we ever be attacked. My second priority is to find planes that will be useful to coalition forces, such as when we provided CF-18s in the fight against Daesh and earlier against the Taliban. How would bush planes be useful in this function?"

The minister of youth rejoined the discussion. "Sir, don't kid yourself. If we are ever attacked, it's likely gonna be by the United States when they want to fully control and exploit our resources. One aircraft carrier has 65 jets, and they have 11 aircraft carriers. And that's just the Naval Air Arm. The Army and the Air Force also have thousands of fighter planes and bombers. So, you are never gonna have enough money to buy enough jets to repel an air invasion should the USA decide to go that route. Excuse me." Danni paused for a sip of water, but it was clear she wasn't done speaking.

"But if you need to placate the jet jockeys currently in our Air Force who dream of dogfights, I'm sure we could mount a 50 cal. on these planes. Sent up in groups of 20, they would be like a group of hummingbirds when threatened by an eagle. The hummingbirds will drive the eagle away with superior numbers. As to your second priority regarding NATO or coalitions missions, we should provide bush planes rather than jets, and use the planes for humanitarian or resupply purposes: delivering food, water and medical supplies to the local people caught in the middle, or delivering bullets, beans and fresh troops to coalition forces on the ground."

Danni Grey Eyes was an emotional, passionate and persuasive speaker when she got on a roll. "Harjit, you did three tours in Kandahar as an infantry and intelligence officer. You told me once that an ISAF jet took off from Kandahar Air Field every minute for 18 months straight. You showed me pictures of American ground crew writing "FREEDOM, courtesy of the USA," on bombs to be dropped on villages unlucky enough to have a bad guy in town. But you also told me how heartsick that made you feel. If we went there to win hearts and minds over to our way of thinking, then we did not succeed by dropping thousands of bombs where we thought the bad guys were. So rather than commit massive amounts to money to buy a few jets, we could spend our money much more effectively by building our own eight- and 12- and 24-seat planes that can serve our country and our allies full time. Then we could show the world that a military force can be used to deliver hope and help."

Danni looked around the room. Less Izmore, who had lost a son to an IED in Kandahar, was wiping away tears and nodding his thanks at her. Harjit Singh was also clearly moved by what Danni had said and by memories of his time—27 months—spent in Kandahar.

"I'm sorry," Danni said, blushing. "I just talked a lot. I'm done. Peace out."

"Danni, please don't ever apologize for saying what's on your mind," Elijah told her. "These are the sort of frank and honest discussions we need to have. Danni? Or Less? What does it cost to build the sort of planes you are talking about?"

"Sir, Viking Air in Victoria has the plans and rights to build de Havilland Beavers and Otters," Less responded. "These are tough little planes that have a 50-year lifespan if well maintained. The more we build, the cheaper they get, but they start at around $500,000 each. If we order more than 5,000, we can get the price down to $425,000 through economy of scale. If we order more than 10,000, that number reduces to…"" Less paused to check his notes. "$315,000."

Elijah and half the people in the room were punching numbers into calculators. "So, the math works," Elijah summarized for the group. "We've had five billion dollars earmarked in the budget for jet replacement. A few years ago, that was gonna buy 72 jets, now it only buys 50 jets, that are gonna get made elsewhere. But for slightly less money we can buy 15,000 bush planes that we can build here with Canadian material and Canadian labour, and that serve a far greater purpose." He checked his watch.

"Harjit, my old friend. As minister of defence you will be the guy selling this idea. So, first, are you comfortable that this is the way to go? And second, who will be the main adversaries or opponents of this plan?"

"Yes, I am confident that this is the right decision," Harjit smiled confidently through his magnificent salt and pepper beard. "As for adversaries, the only ones I anticipate are the conglomerate that builds over-priced jets, and the 300 trained fighter pilots in our Air Force anxiously awaiting new jets. We need not worry about the wealthy few people who build jets. For the latter, I suggest we use our current trained pilots to test these planes during development, and then to train other pilots. There will inevitably be some whining among the Air Force officers that they will now be asked to fly crude bush planes rather than sleek sexy jets." The minister of defence looked grimly determined. "At some point, those pilots who are truly unhappy with their fate may leave and those who truly love to fly will remain."

"All right then. It's showtime," said Canada's highly irregular and unusual prime minister to his ministers, rising from the table. "Let's go speak with our fellow parliamentarians. Once we have heard from our fellow MPs, we can put it to a vote. Questions?"

Niagara Falls, Ontario

Abuela Rosa and Lumpy's Gramma Hanna had quickly become close friends since the Gonzalez Family had moved into her rooming house. There were seven dormitory rooms and three very busy bathrooms in the old Victorian home, which now housed 27 (mostly young) boarders. The guests paid Gramma Hanna $10 a night for a bed, or $20 a night for a bed with breakfast and supper. For $5 more, she would make her guests a packed lunch, but needed to know 24 hours in advance. It was a pretty good deal, especially on Saturday night, because Hanna always served the same menu on Saturday: *barszcz*, then *placki ziemniaczane* and *bigos*, and plenty of *krupnik*. "Dudes, don't even try to say it. Just taste the love," Lumpy used to tell newcomers to Gramma Hanna's house.

"So, Rosa, you help me clean and cook meals six hours a day, and your room and meals are free, plus I pay you twenty dollars a day, no?" Hanna asked Rosa in her strong Polish accent.

"OK," Rosa said. "When I am starting?"

"Now, with breakfast," Hanna replied happily. "But first, we toast new friendship with *krupnik*, yes?'"

Rosa had no idea what Hanna was proposing, and she'd certainly never heard of *krupnik*, but she didn't want to offend her new Canadian friend. Hannah proudly poured them each a generous slug of *krupnik*. "*Sto lat*," Hanna toasted her new friend.

"*Salud*," Rosa replied, clinking Hanna's glass, and following Hanna's lead, bravely draining it. Judging by

Rosa's reaction, *krupnik* was clearly not for the faint of heart.

"Gramma, don't make Rosa drink *krupnik* with you," scolded Lumpy, who just entered the kitchen. "*Abuela*, uuum, Fabiola, tell her be careful. That's my gramma's homemade moonshine." Hanna expertly snapped at her grandson with a tea towel in response as he just as expertly jumped out of the way.

Fabiola laughed and spoke quickly to Rosa, who laughed even harder.

"Lumpy and Hanna, I am like *krupnik*. I make a same drink in my village before we left Guatemala."

"I knew you would like it, Rosa. Is old Polish recipe— potato vodka with honey and secret herbs…"

"It's a secret, all right, because it's illegal," Lumpy interrupted Gramma Hanna. "Fabiola, that's moonshine. It's good for cleaning paintbrushes, or…owwww!" Lumpy yelped as his Gramma's tea towel found its target midthigh with a resounding snap.

"Don't listen to this boy's crazy talk," Hanna told her new friend. "Every day I have *krupnik*, and I am healthy like the horse. Now, please, Rosa, knife, fork, spoon for 27 people, yes?" Hanna slid open a large drawer filled with silverware and did a quick demo of three utensils wrapped in a serviette.

Breakfast was self serve. This morning the crew was having their choice of: coffee or tea, apple juice, oatmeal, yoghurt, milk, rye bread, a ham slice, sliced tomatoes, some goat cheese and bananas.

"So much food," *Abuela* Rosa murmured in Spanish.

Lumpy, T-Bone and eight of their militia friends ate quickly and ran out the door in uniform to catch the 0730 bus to the armory.

The Gonzalez Family, like many migrant workers, had spent the spring, summer and fall following the crops north. As undocumented migrants, they had planted tomatoes in Florida in early March, then cabbage and cauliflower in South Carolina, and tobacco in Virginia in early May. By late August they were in Upstate New York picking peaches, plums, pears, cherries, grapes and apples. Regardless of where they went, however, they never really felt welcomed or appreciated. They knew they were only being paid a small percentage of what white Americans were being paid for the same work.

When times seemed toughest *Abuela* Rosa reminded them that: "It's still better than what we left." The family had once been wealthy. They owned land and operated a thriving coffee export business. Rosa's husband–Guillermo's father–had become politically active and outspoken against increasingly dysfunctional and greedy politicians. Eventually, corrupt officials turned on him, and the family land and fortunes were seized as government assets.

When the Great Canadian Blackout hit, they were volunteering and living in a homeless shelter run by the Salvation Army in Buffalo, New York.

Several days after meeting Lumpy and Gramma Hanna, Guillermo and Valariano began working as herdsmen for an old farmer named Hank Goris. Hank attended Gramma Hanna's church, and she had introduced the Gonzalez Family to the congregation and mentioned that they were looking for work. Hank had 160 goats, but he was getting too old to manage his farm.

"How's them Mexicans working out for ya, Hank?" a clerk asked a few days later at the local hardware store, not even stopping to consider that Guillermo or Valariano might speak or understand English. "I don't have any Mexicans working with me, Jimmy," deadpanned Hank. "Tell him, Guillermo."

"Sir, we are hopeful new Canadians," Guillermo responded proudly, "recently arrived from Guatemala."

"And to answer your question, Jimmy, they're the best people I've ever worked with," Hank added emphatically.

"Oh. See, I heard ya speaking Mexican and just assumed…" Jimmy was proving once again that he only opened his mouth to change feet, and that he was not, by any means, a man accustomed to meeting anyone from outside his circle of influence. (A small circle consisting of local white folk.)

Hank didn't want to give Jimmy any more time to make things worse. "Jimmy, the language you heard Guillermo and Valariano speaking is Spanish, not Mexican. It's spoken in more than 50 countries worldwide," Hank explained as he handed the Gonzalez men the various boxes of nails, wire and staples they had just purchased. "So, the next time you see these gentlemen in your store, please just welcome them the same way you do all your regular customers."

Hank tipped his hat to Jimmy's daughter on his way out the door. "Henrietta."

"Now what do you suppose got him up on his high horse?" Jimmy wondered to Henrietta in a hurt tone, as the three men got in Hank's truck. "Hank and me have been friends since high school …"

"Really?" Henrietta responded. "I was thinking it was your uneducated assumption that all Spanish-speaking people were Mexican, and the fact that you spoke to Hank as if the two men with him weren't even there."

Jimmy knew he was in the wrong but had never been good at admitting it. "Mexican, Spanish, Guatican, whatever. I don't understand why we keep taking all these foreigners in anyways. Things wuz good the way they wuz."

"Holy smokes, Hillbilly Jim. Listen to yourself. 'Things wuz good the way they wuz?' You mean with greedy white baby boomers living a life of unsustainable luxury exploiting the land we stole from First Nations people? Sure, Dad, let's try and protect that way of life," Henrietta responded sarcastically.

"Now, see here, you young people don't appreciate how good you got it," Jimmy responded defensively to his daughter.

"No! Wrong!" his daughter shouted, standing up from her computer, getting angrier. "Most people my age actually do understand how lucky we are to live here, and we are willing to share that high standard of living with other less fortunate people from other less fortunate places. And if you can't understand why that's a good thing, you should at least try not to let your red neck be so visible the next time some people who weren't born here come into your store."

Henrietta made a very definite point of slamming the door that separated her office from the remainder of her father's store. A moment later she noticed her dad was trying to look at the back of his neck in a mirror.

God, if you are out there, please help him, Henrietta sighed as she kept filing sales reports.

While her brother and father worked at the farm, Fabiola had started a business weaving scarves, tablecloths and skirts. Hanna's Church of the Immaculate Conception lent her $1,000 in seed money to buy a used loom and some material. The church also let her set up a workshop in a back room in the church hall. She repaid the money, plus 10 per cent, within six weeks, then started paying rent on the space in the hall, and then hired two ladies from Cote d'Ivoire to help them keep up with demand. "Nuevo Mundo" textiles was a growing concern.

The Church of the Immaculate Conception had been perilously close to the chopping block a year ago. Low attendance getting lower, average age of parishioners dangerously high, too few young people in the church, more funerals than weddings and christenings by a ten to one ratio, rising heat and maintenance costs...

"These are not sustainable numbers," the bishop told Father Jakub on his annual road trip from Hamilton.

"Give us one more year, and we'll have some better numbers for you, Padre," Father Jakub pleaded with the old Irishman.

"Let me think about it," Bishop O'Keefe grumbled.

I guess that's better than an order to begin preparation for deconsecration, Father Jakub thought.

Fortunately for Father Jakub and the Church of the Immaculate Conception, the new Canadian government's immigration policy had been a lifeline. In the past year, the congregation had doubled, and the majority of new parishioners were younger families like the Gonzalez Family. With the new families came new energy. Guillermo played the accordion, and Valariano and Fabiola were amazing singers.

"Can you do *Ave Maria* again this week?" Father Jakub asked them for the third week in a row.

"As you wish, Padre," Guillermo replied.

"You don't think people are getting tired of it?" Fabiola wondered.

"Oh, heavens, no, my child," Father Jakub replied, "It's our congregation that is asking to hear it."

A new family from Ecuador got the choir restarted, first with 11 voices, the next week with 15, the week after, 19…

The several families from Cote d'Ivoire often performed musical numbers as well, in their African-influenced French dialect. Local people who hadn't been to any church in years started coming again (many of them just for the live music, but they didn't tell Father Jakub that…)

"Darkness cannot drive out darkness, only light can do that. Hate cannot drive out hate, only love can do that. Love will conquer hate."
—*Reverend Doctor Martin Luther King*

CHAPTER 6

Viva la Resistance!

Washington DC

PRESIDENT TRIMP IS BACK! trumpeted the *Daily Bugles* of the world.

TRIMP IS POTUS? asked *The Guardian*.

"The Supreme Court of the United States is dropping all charges against President Trimp and the Trimp Administration," Sarah Huckleberry Slanders told the Press Corps in a short, terse statement. "President Trimp is back in the White House where he belongs. He is the rightful president as elected by the American people in 2016. The charges against President Trimp were fabricated by Fake News media outlets. I repeat: the SCOTUS is dropping all charges against the POTUS. There are no facts to support charges of collusion, or treason, or any of the other ridiculous allegations against the president."

"What about the president's recent attempted nuclear launch on Canada?" a CNN reporter asked. "Surely that's a war crime and indicates that Mr. Trimp is mentally unfit to be president?"

"That was merely a test," the press secretary responded bluntly. "President Trimp did a surprise test launch to see if the Chiefs of Staff were capable of exercising good judgement rather than blindly following orders. The president wants you to know he has complete faith in our military leadership."

"Where is Nancy Pillosi?" shouted a reporter from MSNBC.

If looks could kill, that reporter would have died instantly. Sarah Slanders cast a baleful glare from underneath her smoky grey lieshadow at the reporter who had dared to be so insolent.

"I'm afraid that's all the time we have for today," Slanders said in acid tones. She turned on her heels, and stalked out of the room, surrounded by well-armed Team America members.

New York, New York

"Welcome back to Morning Joe. Our headline guest this morning is former First Lady Michelle Oobima, who is attempting to be the first Independent president since George Washington. Mrs. Oobima, what is your reaction to the news that President Trimp is back in the White House?"

"Joe, my initial reactions were all negative," Michelle began. "I felt shock, horror, even betrayal. Shock that our medical experts allowed Mr. Trimp to be released from their care after demonstrating that he is clearly not mentally stable. This man attempted to launch our entire nuclear arsenal at Canada six days ago.

"Next, I felt horrified that our democratic systems, our judiciary, our checks and balances, and the rule of law have degraded to the point where we have a POTUS acting like a dictator. Mr. Trimp has always believed he is above the law. But it's horrific to know that he has corrupted our system into supporting and enabling a dictator who answers to no one."

People (even people who hated him) often (reluctantly) remarked that Barrack Oobima was a gifted orator, a public speaker capable of soaring, of reaching great heights. Michelle was better.

"Joe, I felt betrayed by all three branches of our government. The Executive Branch under Mr. Trimp has acted illegally on many occasions, yet he has not been held accountable by the Legislative and Judicial branches of our government.

"So, Joe, those were my 'initial' reactions to the news that Mr. Trimp is once again in the White House claiming to be president. I believe his release yesterday was illegal and unconstitutional. I believe that Mr. Trimp and Russian President Vladimir Poutine worked together in a coordinated effort to sway the outcome of the election in 2016 in Donald Trimp's favour."

Michelle was clear, calm, defiant, passionate. It was obvious she was both angry and yet still in control of that anger. The camera swung in for a close-up.

"Joe, listen. In my heart, I have always believed that Donald Trimp is a liar, a criminal, a bully and a thug. He has brought out the worst in all of us. From the White House he has used hatred and lies to divide us as a people. I have never called Donald Trimp 'my president' and I never will, because I believe he won the election in 2016 illegally, with interference from Russia. He has corrupted, defiled, tarnished, and tainted the presidency, our democracy, and all our sacred institutions. I believe that the majority of American people agree with me. So, I'm asking them to participate in democracy. America needs your help this November. We need you to study the issues and challenges that face our country. Then we need you to vote for the persons who can best address those issues and challenges."

"Mrs Oobima…"

"Joe, please call me Michelle."

"Michelle, what is the biggest obstacle the Independent party faces in the upcoming election?"

"Well, by far the biggest obstacle is getting our candidates' names on the ballot. It should be a simple process, but it isn't. You see, Democratic and Republican nominees are automatically placed on every ballot. But it is a dogfight to get any other name on that ballot. So, in each state and in every district, we have had to fight very hard against incredibly complex bureaucratic regulations. Republicans and Democrats simply don't want Americans to have more than two choices on a ballot. Our Independent candidates' applications are being routinely 'lost,' or 'misplaced' or being sent to higher offices for 'further review.' The Republican and Democratic parties have secretly colluded for years to make the application process very difficult–next to impossible even–for everyone other than their candidates."

"You are saying that the two traditional parties have secretly colluded to protect this…duopoly, I believe you called it?" Joe asked.

"Of course, they have. It's a win-win for both of them. The Federal Election Commission are the most corrupt political hacks in the country. The commission is made up of three loyal Democrats and three loyal Republicans. Their prime function is to protect the duopoly they currently enjoy, and to make it very difficult for any third-party members to get their names on any ballot," Michelle said.

She paused for a second and added, "You heard the FEC chairman's response when I accused them of wilfully obstructing the American people from exercising their democratic freedom of choice, yes?" Michelle asked.

"It's just out this morning. Let's roll the tape."

A Republican commissioner from Wyoming responded (unaware that it was being taped). "Mrs. Oobima, if you like the multi-party system so much, then you should move to Sri Lanka or India or some other shithole that has that system. This is America. People have two choices here: Democrat or Republican."

The camera swung back to the host, Joe Scarbro. "So Mrs Oobi…, sorry, Michelle, how many Independent names are currently on ballots?"

"There are 113. The remainder—the other 355—of our Independent applications are lost or under review, or have been shredded," Michelle Oobima replied indignantly.

"So as the leader of the Independent People's Party, how do you propose to overcome this challenge?"

"Joe, I'm glad you asked that question," the former FLOTUS began as the camera zoomed in on her again. "Because I believe the American people want to have more than two choices in this year's election. So, we are organizing 'Resistance Rallies' at every state capitol building, a rally in every city with more than half a million people, and a rally at the White House, beginning tomorrow morning at 8 o'clock local time." Michelle was controlled but also righteously indignant.

"And we are going to ask that every American who wants to have true democratic freedom to attend one of these peaceful protests. I want to stress: these will be peaceful protests, and that we are within our rights to lawfully assemble in these locations. Our website, www.IndependentParty.com, has all the info people should need if they want to be well informed."

"How long do you expect these rallies to last?" the host queried.

"Until our elected officials do the right thing and order every state and district to put Independent candidates' names on ballots."

EveryTown, USA

The turnout for Resistance Rallies the following day all across the USA was staggering. Mind blowing. Apocalyptic.

There were 1.3 million people at or around the National Mall by 11 a.m. Gridlock. The nation's capital was paralyzed. Again.

An estimated 225,000 people were at the capitol buildings in Bismarck, North Dakota. "Despite the extreme cold, 30 per cent of our state's population has gathered around our capitol building," a young reporter told CBS viewers. "And we are not leaving!" shouted a young man with a bundled-up baby. "We, the people! We, the people!" the crowd was chanting.

It was a big crowd for any city, but for Bismarck? "Well, we've never seen anything like this up here in North Dakota," the governor was saying.

Florida, New York, Texas, Ohio, Illinois, Ohio, Michigan, Georgia, Pennsylvania and California–the most populated states–did their rallies a little differently. Rather than just paralyze a state capitol with a peaceful demonstration, "The Resistance" in these populous states were organized in every major centre with more than 500,000 people.

Many factories and places of business didn't open or were closed by noon. Most main city thoroughfares were blocked with a massive crush of people. The CEO of Starbucks (who was running as an Independent senator) offered his employees double time if they came to work and gave their coffee free to anyone while supplies lasted. Not to be outdone, Dunkin' Donuts, Pizza Hut, McDonald's, Burger King, Subway and many, many other food service corporations quickly followed suit, offering some kind of "Resistance Deal."

"We are kind-hearted people," Michelle Oobima told a reporter in Washington, "and the American people have long memories. We won't forget these companies who help us out during the Resistance Rallies."

Food truck operators and hot dog carts were shattering sales records. The Red Cross was setting up medical sites at every rally. Coca-Cola, Nestle and Pepsi were racing to see who could give away the most bottled water.

Of course, not everyone approved of the Resistance Rallies. A machine shop owner in Tuscaloosa, Alabama, threatened to fire any of his employees who attended the rallies. All 76 of his workers quit.

Zealous evangelists who trusted in "Republican Jesus" threw thunderbolts from their actual, TV and Twitter pulpits, crying out that "the rallies were an abomination," and that "true believers must trust in our elected officials."

Various hate groups like the KKK, neo-Nazis, Westboro Baptist Church, Holocaust deniers, neo-Confederates, Redneck Rebels, Michigan Militia, Christian Identity, anti-LGBT, anti-Muslim, anti-immigration, skinheads, Rednecks for Jesus, and the United American Hill Billy Club of America (to list just a few) did their best to break up the rallies by hoisting hateful signs and screaming venomous slogans at those marching.

The Resistance had been well briefed. "Haters gonna hate," the website had warned them. "Don't engage haters. Don't argue with haters. Do not feed their hate. Do feel free to videotape them or take photos of them. If you believe their actions are a hate crime, photos or video footage will be helpful in prosecuting those people.

"Remember what Dr. Martin Luther King said. 'Darkness cannot drive out darkness, only light can do that. Hate cannot drive out hate, only love can do that. Love will conquer hate.'"

Many rallies were marred by violence. In Jackson, Mississippi, the KKK dragged two young black girls into an alley. The protestors pulled the girls out, but not without bloodshed. The girls were shaken badly, 17 people died, and hundreds of people were injured in the melee that followed. Many of the KKK members had brought weapons: hammers, blackjacks, brass knuckles, bats, pick handles, knives...

The Mississippi National Guard and local police used tear gas, fire hoses, dogs and batons to subdue the crowd, and arrested hundreds of The Resistance. They had to arrest 21 of their own Guardsmen who refused to follow orders to fire tear gas into a crowd of seniors.

Unfortunately, that scene was repeated to some degree in numerous American cities. Detroit, Pittsburgh, Philadelphia, Chicago, Jacksonville, Mobile, Little Rock, Houston, Indianapolis, Atlanta...

Four hours into the rallies, America was completely shut down. An estimated 70 million people were marching across the USA. Airports were closed. Buses and trains weren't running. Schools were closed nationwide. University campuses were empty. Hospitals, prisons, police stations, military bases, TV stations, newspapers and restaurants were doing a booming business.

Michelle Oobima addressed the nation at noon, but she spoke directly to President Donald Trimp. "Mr. Trimp, the American people are speaking. They want to have the freedom to choose their elected officials. You somehow currently occupy the office of President of the United States of America. Our request is simple. Give the American people what they want. Allow Independent politicians to run in the next election without obstruction. We are prepared to peacefully protest for as long as it takes. Mr. President, this ball is in your court."

The response from the POTUS was swift and decisive. It came in the form of a presidential address that was also seen around the world. The makeup crew hadn't done him any favours. To hundreds of millions of viewers, Donald Trimp looked like an enraged orange lunatic. His eyes were erratic, unfocused.

It was easy to tell what professional speechwriters had written for Trimp. It was also easy to discern when Trimp strayed from his written notes to give voice to his own thoughts.

"Good afternoon. I have a message for 'The Resistance.' That's a stupid name, by the way. And that's why very few people are attending your ridiculous rallies. Anyway, the current rallies—which are very small and pathetic, and not nearly as big as my rallies—are unlawful, as they pose a danger to public safety for real Americans. Therefore, I order the traitors attending those rallies to disperse immediately, and peacefully return to their homes. In one hour, those lowlife scum who insist on protesting unlawfully will be arrested. These 'Cryin' Resisters' are posing a clear and present danger to our decent American way of life, to our system of democracy and to our public safety. Due to the sheer size of these crowds—which the Fake News has lied about—our proud professional law enforcement agencies can no longer safely maintain public order and peace. Therefore, as of this moment, and by the power and authority vested in me as the commander in chief of the United States of America, I declare that this country is now under martial law. I order 'The Resistance…' (Trimp used the Dr. Evil quotation mark fingers here) "…to disperse, or you will be arrested. You have 57 minutes to break it up."

"I have just come back from the United States, where Canada is having an unaccustomed moment in the spotlight. Once, Canada was the great blank space on the map above the 49th Parallel where the cold weather came from. Now it is seen by many Americans as a beacon of light in a darkening world—a place you might escape to if things get too negative south of the border: still welcoming, still kindly, still pluralistic and committed to fairness. We need to remember that, and to hold our country to the standards it likes to believe it believes in. But nonetheless, at the moment, it shines, at least by comparison. 'As Canadian as possible under the circumstances' used to be a joke. Now it's a hope. Yes, Canada. Be as Canadian as possible. Under the circumstances. And good luck."
—Margaret Atwood, 2018

CHAPTER 7

Your Grampa Had the Biggest Wacek...

Springfield and St. Jacobs, Ontario

The Magic Bus was a 1996 Blue Bird school bus that the Cabinet ministers had purchased for road trips. They paid a community college environmental conversion class $6,700 to make it run on an electric motor. It could be plugged in to recharge, but the roof and sides of the bus were covered with photovoltaic panels that charged the battery bank. On each corner of the bus roof was a small windmill. Those four small windmills also charged the bus batteries. Danni Grey Eyes and Charley Shackleton had both been school bus drivers back in the day.

It was the inaugural road trip for the Magic Bus. The intent was to visit 40 new environmentally sustainable projects in Ontario, Quebec, New Brunswick, Nova Scotia and Newfoundland over the next 40 days, and do a similar Western swing in the fall.

"Charley!"

"What?" came the muffled reply from the upstairs bathroom in the farmhouse.

"The Magic Bus is here!"

"OK, I'll be right down," Charley hollered to his new bride Dorothy. They had been married for almost a year, but to anyone who met them, they still carried on like newlyweds. "Any problem with the list of chores?" he was asking as he carried a suitcase down the stairs. "Do you have Bob's number in case you need help?"

"No, and yes. And I don't anticipate needing any help, but if I do I'll call Bob Boughner. Listen, you need to stop worrying about me," Dorothy replied. "I'm a SimpleTown girl, Charley Shackleton. I was born to run a farm like this," she continued, showing her husband a lean, muscled bicep. "Now go. Fred and I have got this covered."

"Woof," Fred agreed.

Dorothy pushed Charley out the door and went out with him to speak with the group on the Magic Bus. It was a bright, sunny, winter day in Elgin County. The sun was bouncing off the fresh snow that had fallen the night before, which doubled the blinding brightness of the day. Most of the ministers, and about half a dozen journalists, were outside stretching their legs, and admiring Charley's flock, which had left the chicken coop, and were preening themselves in the sun.

"C'mon, people. We can't stand out here all day countin' Charley's chickens. We got a country to visit!" shouted Elijah.

Danni Grey Eyes turned the Magic Bus around slowly in Charley's barnyard. She beeped the horn happily as they turned north on Highway 52. In response, a rooster crowed, Fred barked, and Dorothy blew kisses.

As the bus got underway, Less Ismore stood up to address the crew on board. "OK, people, our next stop is in about 80 minutes in St. Jacobs, just outside Kitchener. This is an Amish community that has recently begun training people in their simple and sustainable way of life."

"The Amish people are the original Simpletons," Less added, "and I mean Simpleton in the most complimentary way," he added for the benefit of any journalists hearing the term for the first time. "These folks have never used electricity, or any other labour-saving devices. The farms we are going to visit have never been worked by tractors, and the land has never been sprayed with any chemical fertilizers or pesticides. They have an absolute treasure trove of knowledge that they are willing now to share with those of us who are willing to learn. The Amish people are very friendly, and they use the Holy Bible as their textbook.

"Listen carefully to these next points," Less stated, again looking pointedly at the journalists on the bus. "They don't like to be photographed for religious reasons, so please don't try to sneak any photos of them. Out of respect, let's turn our phones off, and keep them in our pockets during our visit. Second point of order: we are going to be taken on a tour of their community in their horse-drawn wagons. Then, our hosts have offered to feed us lunch. During the meal, the men and boys will all be seated at long communal tables. The Amish ladies will serve us, and then all the ladies will dine. For our ladies on the bus, I think the Amish ladies won't mind if you help serve. Again, out of respect for our hosts' customs and traditions, I'm gonna ask that the ladies on the bus stay with the Amish ladies, and the men stay with the menfolk. Let's not try to break new ground for the women's liberation movement in this community. Trust me, they are not ready to receive that message, and they may react by not welcoming back more visitors. Third point: the Amish people don't practise politics. They don't vote, other than to select their elders. They don't watch TV, read papers or listen to the radio. These folks have no dealing with the outside world. They don't attend our schools—they have their own. When speaking with them, just use your name. They aren't gonna understand a position title like prime minister or senator. Questions?"

There were none. Juliette plugged in a CD, and most of the Magic Bus passengers worked on tablets, phones or notebooks, or chatted quietly among themselves.

"Two minutes till showtime, people," Danni announced after the bus has passed through some gently rolling countryside. The Magic Bus turned into a large yard, where at least 30 horse and buggies were tied to a split-rail fence. One of the younger Amish men waved them into a parking spot clearly reserved for the Magic Bus. Once parked, Danni opened the door, and he entered the bus. "Good day to you all," he addressed the crowd on the bus, in what seemed like Olde English. "My name is Elmo Stoll. Welcome to St. Jacobs. May God's blessings be upon us all today. Please, come and meet our elders," he encouraged with a gesture.

The visitors stepped off the bus and were warmly greeted by five elders. "It's like the receiving line when meeting the governor general," Juliette whispered to Elijah. It took several minutes for the visitors to be warmly greeted by the elders.

"Please, this way," Elmo was saying. He explained as they walked together, "Today, we have perfect weather to show you our community. First, we are building an addition to our school. As we begin to welcome more people to our community, we need a place where we can speak and share knowledge with our visitors." At the back of the school, approximately 40 Amish men, all clad exactly the same in black, and most sporting beards (but not moustaches) smiled and nodded politely at their guests. A floor of a large building was in place, made of hand-hewn pine planks two inches thick, with one wall standing and braced. Some were shaping beams with adzes. A few more were shaping wooden pegs with drawknives, while others were fitting together the next wall section using hand-chiselled mortise and tenon joinery.

The guests mingled in with their hosts, admiring skills that had been passed down through generations. "Yakub, we have here a wall we might raise?"

"Yes, Elmo. This gable end is ready for raising," Yakub replied proudly.

"For our visitors who wish to help, please raise your hands." Every hand went up. "Wonderful. The first 10 people here go with Elmo and take up the three ropes," Yakub directed, as the 10 visitors joined a dozen Amish men on the ropes. "And then we will take two people here on each upright," as he walked and talked, and put people in the appropriate positions.

"As we count together to three, the people on the uprights will push up, and those on the ropes will pull, yes? One…two…three." Together, the Amish hosts and their guests counted, then raised a section of wall 60 feet long and 24 feet high. "Now, we hold the wall in place," Yakub directed as a group of the younger Amish men quickly secured the new wall to the other wall with wooden pegs and braces. "All is secure, Yakub!" a man shouted. The guests applauded and hooted and shook the hands of the nearest Amish men.

"Now, next, we will ask our guests to board this sleigh, yes?" Elmo was saying. The sleigh had 20 bales of hay in the middle, and the guests sat around the outside. In front of the sleigh were six of the largest and most beautiful Clydesdale horses any of the guests had ever seen, shaking their heads, and snorting, eager to get to work. An Amish man lifted the reins and spoke softly in German. The six horses pulled together as one, and the sleigh began to glide out of the barnyard.

"So, we will go to another farm for a visit," Elmo was explaining as he sat among the guests. "We will drop off this hay, and then return with some lumber." Elmo continued to play the role of tour guide, explaining the simple principles of crop rotation, the need for ground to rest in a fallow state, the advantages of doing work by hand and horsepower. As former farmers who strove to be Simpletons, Charley and Less asked the most questions. Danni and Benjamin huddled together for warmth, as did Juliette and Elijah.

They offloaded the hay in the Hiltz barn, and Mr. Israel Hiltz and his six sons helped load the lumber, then jumped on board with the guests. The boys were four, five, seven, nine, 12 and 15 years old. Their eyes were sky blue, and their hair (under matching black hats) was the blondest blonde Juliette had ever seen. "Hello," she said, sliding between the boys. "I'm Juliette, and this is my friend Elijah." She and Elijah made a point of shaking each boy's hand as they turned beet red and looked shyly at their feet.

The horses pulled the sleigh back into the barnyard, where another section of wall had just been raised, and school had let out. "Now, we are hoping that everyone is hungry. Please, if the men will come this way," Elmo directed. "And if the ladies will please join Mrs. Yoder."

Mrs. Yoder and the other Amish women and girls approached the ladies warmly. The Mennonite ladies all wore black bonnets, and severe black ankle-length dresses over granny boots. The young Mennonite girls especially were quite wide eyed at meeting someone like Juliette, with her massive 70s Afro, and Danni Grey Eyes, who was dressed like an Indian princess with a braid of raven black hair down to her hips.

The ladies went into a large communal kitchen, on the back of the building the men had just entered, where things smelled amazing.

"Can we please help you serve the men?" Juliette asked on behalf of the guests.

"Of course," Mrs. Yoder replied, relieved that they had asked. She peered out a door into a large barn-like space where her husband was giving thanks in German. "Amen," said the men all together, when he had finished.

The ladies sprung into action. Mrs. Yoder directed traffic. Each of the ladies was given a platter, or large bowl, and told, "There at table one, there at table two, there at table three," and so forth. The platters were laid by the elder at each table who took a portion and passed the platter to his right. The Mennonite men and boys over four, and their visitors, waited patiently at three trestle tables, each table with approximately 35 men.

Smoked pork hocks, baked apples, salt beef short ribs, sauerkraut, *spaetzle*, roasted potatoes, German-fried cabbage, pickled green beans, cauliflower salad, fresh bread, fresh butter, smoked cheese, fresh milk... and shoofly pie with tea at the end. The visitors noticed that their hosts didn't speak while dining, so the meal was a quiet, but massively enjoyable affair.

After the ladies had served the men, they themselves dined in groups of 30, with another group minding the children, and the third group keeping an eye on the men folk.

When the meal had concluded, Elijah asked Elmo, "Can we speak to your whole community together? We'd like a chance to thank everyone for the hospitality you have shown us today."

After a brief conference with the elders, Elmo returned, smiling. "Of course. We'll bring the ladies and children in."

Abraham Yoder was speaking to his wife in the kitchen, who then marshalled the Amish ladies, children and female guests into the room. The male visitors in the dining room stood and began to applaud, followed somewhat timidly by their Amish counterparts.

When all the ladies were in the room, Elijah stepped out front. "Brothers and Sisters," he began, thank you all so very, very much for the kindness and loving spirit that you have shared with us today..." He paused for applause (mostly from the guests). "Thank you for the most delicious meal. We recognize that this is a total community effort..." more applause, "...and tremendous thanks for having the courage to accept outsiders into your community, and for sharing the very valuable customs and traditions that you believe in." Elijah was pacing slowly now, like a cool black panther, addressing everyone in the room. "Unfortunately, we must leave in a few moments." *awwwwwwwwwwwww* (from the guests), "So again, thank you, thank you–a thousand times–thank you."

The whole community was out to see the Magic Bus off. The men had raised the fourth wall of the new building and were boarding up the roof with their own planks milled at Brother Israel's farm. The Amish ladies had loaded up a massive packed lunch for the travellers.

Brother Elmo and the elders boarded the bus last to say goodbye. Brother Yakub said a prayer in Old German, then Brother Abraham in English.

Elmo Stoll spoke last. "Our elders want me to tell you. We understand that you are the elected elders and shepherds of this country. And Canada welcomed us many years ago when our people were fleeing religious persecution. We are grateful that we are free to live among you and practise our way of life without interference." Brother Elmo paused to gather his thoughts. "We also understand that we have much to learn from each other. If you can be patient with us, we are willing to slowly, slowly accept more people from outside our community to visit with us, and to share our knowledge. You see, despite our different customs and traditions, we believe that we are all God's children. Therefore, we ask for God's blessing on your journey, as you go to visit your flock."

Niagara Falls, Ontario

After forming government, the Independent People's Party had quickly passed legislation aimed at increasing immigration to Canada and encouraging Canadians to move back to rural areas and operate farms. The Pioneer Program offered successful applicants up to 20 acres of Crown land if the applicants agreed to use the land in a productive and sustainable manner. A similar program of land grants had been used very successfully in the 1920s and 1930s to attract immigrants to Canada. For recent arrivals like the Gonzalez Family, the Pioneer Program was an opportunity to own land and use the skills they had learned in Guatemala to support themselves.

However, the Gonzalez Family had recently withdrawn its application to the Pioneer Program for a much more appealing offer. The farmer they had been working for, Hank Goris, was turning over ownership of his farm to the family.

"You just gotta promise to let me live here as long as I can. And, you gotta promise to live here with me." The family tried for a week to refuse the offer as being too generous, but Hank would hear none of it. "Look, I have no children," Hank told them. "I've been alone since my wife died last year. If your family doesn't take this farm, I'll just sell it and go be lonely and bored somewhere," he threatened. "You're doing me the favour. I know that you will treat the farm well, and I get to enjoy the company of your family in my declining years."

The farm included 90 acres of prime Niagara Valley farmland, a woodlot, 160 goats (and accompanying lucrative milk quota), two barns and a ramshackle farmhouse.

Fabiola's business, Nuevo Mundo textiles, was also expanding. Fabiola Gonzalez was a shrewd but fair business woman and a very hard worker. The company produced top-quality tablecloths at first and quickly expanded its product line to include beautiful wall hangings, quilts and heavy Guatemalan-style shirts and hoodies made by hand from hemp, cotton (and soon, Nubian wool.)

The Gonzalez Family had also inspired about 50 new parishioners to begin attending the Church of the Immaculate Conception in the past few months.

Bishop O'Keefe came to visit in February. The bishop was not a man who wore his emotions on his sleeve—most people who met O'Keefe described him as a "grumpy old man"—but he was pleasantly surprised with the increased attendance and energy in the tiny parish. It was one of the more diverse and colourful parishes in the diocese. The people's responses to the priest's Order of Mass were heard in Polish, Dutch, Spanish, Creole, French and English.

"Dude, it's awesome here in the House of God," Lumpy told the bishop on the way out after Mass. "All these people just getting high on Jesus. It's a beautiful thing."

Guillermo, Valariano and Fabiola were staying after Mass to practise with the choir, so Lumpy drove Gramma Hanna's old car back from church.

"I see you talking to the bishop after Mass," Gramma Hanna teased her grandson. "Did you think to confession for impure thoughts about Fabiola?"

Lumpy blushed. "My impure thoughts are that obvious?"

Hanna laughed, then shrugged. "Fabiola is beautiful girl. You are boy. Boys like beautiful girls. Is normal, Rosa, yes?"

From the backseat Rosa agreed. "*Si. Fabiola es muy bonita*. But you should ask the father if you want to dating her. Guatemaltecos are still old school like that." Rosa's English was improving, even if she was learning improper grammar from her best buddy Hanna. Both Hanna's and Rosa's language were oddly peppered with common phrases they had recently learned from their young guests at the boarding house.

"Gramma, she is way outta my league."

"Yeah, that's what your grandfather thinked before his friends talked him into asking me out," Gramma Hanna reminisced mistily. "Did you know your grampa had the biggest *wacek* in our village? I still lose my breathing thinking about it…"

"Gramma, please, we don't wanna hear about how big grampa's *wacek* was…"

"Speak for yourself," cackled Rosa from the backseat. "I'm always liking a good *wacek* story."

An eye for an eye will make the whole world blind.
—*Mahatma Gandhi*

CHAPTER 8

Dark Days and Darker Nights

Everywhere, USA

As President Trimp had promised, at 1400 local time, police forces and members of the National Guard and United States Armed Forces began to arrest people at the Resistance Rallies. In Augusta, Bangor and Portland, Maine, some 1,700 people were arrested by nightfall. An estimated 1,200 protesters were arrested in Concord, New Hampshire, over the same period. Sen. Barney Saunders had flown home to Vermont to be with his constituents. He was the first person arrested on the steps of the capitol building in Montpelier. The billions of people who saw the video agreed, he wasn't resisting arrest. In fact, like a wild-haired Gandhi, he had just been telling the crowd to "remain calm. Don't fight back if you are being arrested" through a megaphone as the police and military forces arrived in riot gear.

His arrest was remarkably brutal. He was slammed face first into the stone steps of the building, and one officer knelt on the back of his neck while a second officer zap strapped his hands behind his back. "The rest of you peace-niks should clear out!" a deputy shouted at them through the megaphone he had slapped out of Barney's hand. "Or you are gonna get a dose of the same medicine." Some people dispersed, but the greater majority stayed, and despite their peaceful behaviour, many were arrested in the same unnecessarily brutal manner as Barney Saunders.

Shit got a lot crazier in the bigger cities. Police forces and troops were using fire hoses, tear gas and batons to disperse the crowds in Boston. "I don't have enough manpower or cells to arrest and hold this many lawbreakers," a state trooper captain with a hawhd Boston accent was telling a reporter. "America is under martial law by order of the president of the United States. So, we are encouraging these people to disperse. It's January here in Massachusetts. Do you wanna be sprayed with a fire hose or tear gas? If not, go home. Cold water and tear gas seem to help people make their minds up. Those people who don't disperse are gonna be arrested."

As if to prove his point, the TV crew recorded officers wading into a group of dozens of people who had been sprayed with tear gas, but still refused to leave. Their arms were linked together, so they were being hit on the head with riots sticks until their arms went up in self-defence. As they raised their arms, they were pulled out of the group, thrown on their faces, arrested and hauled away in amazing numbers.

"Where are the people arrested being held?" the reporter asked the captain.

"Fenway Paahwk," the captain replied.

"But it's below freezing, there is rain in the forecast and Fenway Park is an uncovered unheated stadium," the reporter cried in apparent horror.

"That's true. But all our regular cells are full, so these people should probably go home, or spend a very cold night in Fenway. Oh, and the Red Sox don't play there till April in case people are thinking it might be fun."

"Why not use TD Gardens where the Bruins and Celtics play?" the reporter wondered. "At least it's heated."

"Look, if we make things too comfortable, we'll have to arrest half the people in Boston," was the captain's infamous response.

Baltimore, Washington, Trenton, New York City, Norfolk, Philadelphia, Charleston, Jacksonville, Miami… all turned ugly early. Resistance protesters clashed with police from the very beginning, for the first minute with their bare hands. When the police began using riot sticks, rubber bullets and tear gas, a few resistors in each of these cities fired back with handguns. Panic ensued on both sides. While 99.99 per cent of the crowd was unarmed, many were shot in the panic and madness that ensued.

As the rallies/riots were going down, so was a lot of vandalism in many cities. Whether it was by resisters, or YUDs (Young Urban Destroyers) masquerading as resisters was unclear. Shop windows were being kicked in and the stores subsequently looted. Police cars and government vehicles were being flipped and set on fire, police stations and government buildings were being firebombed with Molotov cocktails. By 1200 Pacific Standard Time, the entire United States of America—from Portland, Maine, to Portland, Oregon—was officially out of control.

President Donald Trimp was alone in a secure meeting room in the Pentagon getting ready for a brief from his advisors, as the White House was deemed too difficult to defend. "We can keep you and your team safer here, Sir," his security detail had told him. *Fifteen minutes before my meeting with advisors.* He found a remote and the TV flickered to life.

"This is Malcolm Furness for BBC1 World News. Good evening. Our lead story tonight: Crisis in America. As most viewers are aware, last night the former and current American President Donald Trimp declared that the USA was under martial law. Yesterday Trimp stated, "Martial Law is essential to protect American citizens during the rallies planned by persons attempting to destroy democracy and freedom." He went on to say, "America is the cradle of democracy, the birthplace of freedom, and I am the greatest POTUS of all time."

The venerable Mr. Furness continued, with a bar graph appearing on the screen behind him. "Prior to 2020, America already held an unfortunate and embarrassing record: the highest percentage of incarcerated citizens in the world. According to census figures in 2019, 2.5 million Americans, or 1.1 per cent of American citizens, were in prison. After seven hours of Resistance Rallies, 2.6 million more Americans have been arrested and are currently imprisoned, many in sub-zero outdoor ball parks and football stadiums. Their apparent crime is "unlawful assembly, as contained in the regulations surrounding Martial Law." Additionally, over 61 police officers have been reported killed, and more than 3,000 citizens have died, according to our latest sources. It is extremely important for viewers to recall that the Resistance Rallies were started as a means to put pressure on the United States government to put Independent politicians on the ballots in the upcoming election in November."

Furness switched gears and moved to a new story. "To New York now, where the United Nations Secretary-General, Ingrid Aldisdottir, issued a strong and clear condemnation of the US government's actions today, calling the arrests "one of the worst examples of human rights violations seen this century." The secretary-general also offered the US government up to 200,000 UN peacekeepers, with a firm commitment of peacekeepers from: Turkey, Australia, Pakistan, Haiti, Indonesia, Chad, Niger, Egypt, Norway, Ireland, Colombia and Canada."

The respected British newscaster had more to add: "The secretary-general went on to say that the United Nations would consider the strongest possible sanctions against the United States unless the recently arrested protesters were released, and the Resistance Rallies allowed to continue without government interference."

Trimp turned the TV off. He could watch Fox News all day long, but he was unable to stomach the relentless criticism doled out by other American networks or the international press. Lately he had been tuning in BBC

World News, hoping to find a friend or marginally balanced coverage.

Is there anything worse than being mocked and criticized by the British, he wondered?

Trimp consulted his briefing points from Homeland Security. No good news there. Multiple police agencies at the municipal, state and federal level were reporting that officers were refusing orders to arrest citizens and were being arrested themselves in a show of solidarity with the resistance. The report also identified that there weren't enough law enforcement officers or holding facilities to arrest any more people. The main recommendation in his briefing was that those protesters currently being held should be released ASAP because "they could not be safely detained. We do not have the resources in place to hold this number of people without fatalities from overcrowding, exposure, dehydration or starvation, blah, blah, blah," the president read out loud.

He crumpled the paper after reading less than half of it and tried for a three-point shot in a trash can five feet away.

Next, he reviewed his daily briefing notes from the Joint Chiefs of Staff. The main body of the report was similar to the brief from Homeland Security. Approximately 15 per cent of the country's military members–many of them senior officers–were refusing orders to arrest protesters and were instead willing to be arrested themselves for disobeying direct orders.

Attached at the end of the briefing note were the letters of resignation from his Joint Chiefs of Staff : Gen. "Pit Bull" Pruitt, Chief of Staff for the Army; Gen. Germaine Saxon, Chief of Staff for the USAF; Adm. Richard McHale,

Chief of Staff for the USN; and Gen. "Spike" Jones, Chief of Staff for the USMC. *Cowards.*

Trimp crumpled their letters of resignation into another ball of paper. "Trimp, from half court," he announced to himself. "He sinks it! Donald Trimp sinks a three pointer at the buzzer to win the world championships alone, by himself, and the crowd goes wild!"

"Mr. President, your advisors are ready to begin. Shall I send them in?" an executive assistant was wondering. She stooped to pick up eight or nine balls of crumpled paper. The closest was three feet away from the waste basket.

"Please, let's begin," Trimp responded presidentially, assuming his power seat at the head of the table.

Trimp's few advisors and key secretaries (most of whom were blood relatives or long-time business partners) filed in, chattering happily amongst themselves.

Just a few days ago, on her first day in office, former President Nancy Pillosi had fired all the appointments that Trimp had made.

"Trimp's appointments were invalid, as Mr. Trimp is being tried for treason, conspiracy, money laundering, tax evasion, sexual assault, obstruction of justice, et cetera," President Pillosi had stated.

"Welcome back, Team Trimp," The Donald said magnanimously, arms outstretched like a modern-day messiah. "Are you guys ready to MAGA again?" Trimp led his own applause as Don Jr, Ivanka, Eric and Jared joined in enthusiastically.

"All right, listen. Here's my plan, and it's just the best ever." Trimp smiled smugly while his children and the other appointees applauded warmly.

"Now a few days ago, 'Cryin & Lyin Nancy' fired all of you wonderful, bright, talented people."

"She said mean things about you as well, Daddy," Ivanka pouted petulantly.

"She sure did, pumpkin. And what did Daddy always tell you to do to people who are mean to us?"

"Hit them back ten times as hard!" the Trimp trio responded gleefully.

"Exactly. See, we need to hit back more bigly than Nancy did, Mike," Trimp instructed his robotic and loyal VP. "We're not gonna just fire her people. We'll jail them and charge them with conspiracy, or…something. It'll be terrific—trust me. Get our best people in Team America on that ASAP, Mike."

Vice President Pens whispered in a Team America officer's ear. The officer snapped to attention, smartly saluted the president, and marched smartly out of the room.

The Trimp trio applauded their dad's bold manoeuvre. Trimp waved off their applause as though it embarrassed him. (It clearly did not.) A few seconds of applause might have been all right, but Eric showed no sign of slowing down.

Now it's getting weird, Trimp thought.

"All right. Stop. Cut it out. Eric, stop clapping now!" Eric Trimp looked crestfallen. But only for a minute.

"Next, we have the international Fake News media portraying us as monsters, and the 'failing and useless' United Nations threatening sanctions unless we release these traitorous protestors. What I want to hear from you are ideas that allow us a graceful exit from this mess without giving into these radical Independent thingys. We need to show the world that the United States will not be blackmailed."

Every hand in the room went up.

"Ivanka. Whattya got, pumpkin?"

"Innovation is the result of a process that brings radical ideas to create positive change.
—Natasha Tsakos

CHAPTER 9

Some Radical Proposals

As the Magic Bus headed towards its next stop, Elijah checked the updated bullet-point briefing notes his executive assistant always had ready for him and the other members of Cabinet.

"You need to be aware of the top five things going in the world at any given time," Moneypenny had suggested when they were establishing how to best manage his time.

"How would I ever stay focused without you?" Elijah asked his executive assistant shortly after he'd become prime minister.

"I suspect you'd hire another tyrannical taskmaster with similar qualities," she sighed dryly without looking up from her keyboard.

BRIEFING NOTE

1. USA NOW UNDER MARTIAL LAW / AMERICAN ECONOMY / BUSINESSES SHUT DOWN. CONSTITUTIONAL CRISIS LOOMING.

2. RESISTANCE RALLIES ONGOING, LARGEST QUIET REVOLUTION IN HISTORY–120 MILLION PROTESTING.
3. 2.5 MILLION AMERICAN PROTESTERS IN PRISON, INCLUDES POLITICIANS, POLICE AND MILITARY MEMBERS.
4. UNITED NATIONS HQ RELOCATING TO GENEVA (TEMPORARILY?)–EMERGENCY MEETING SCHEDULED TOMORROW TO DISCUSS HUMAN RIGHTS VIOLATIONS AND POSSIBLE UN RESPONSES / PEACEKEEPERS? YOU SHOULD STRONGLY CONSIDER ATTENDING AND PRESENTING THE PEACEKEEPER PLAN THAT MINISTER OF DEFENCE HAS BEEN WORKING ON.
5. FLOODING IN CENTRAL INDIA CAUSING STATE OF EMERGENCY–OFFER DISASTER ASSISTANCE RESPONSE TEAM?
6. YOU SHOULD CONSIDER TELLING JULIETTE HOW BEAUTIFUL SHE LOOKS TODAY (NOTE: I WAS COERCED INTO ADDING THIS…)

Elijah looked up to see Juliette and Moneypenny smiling at him over the back of their bus seats.

"You are both delightful creatures," he said, "without whom I would be eternally lost." He leaned forward to give them both a peck on the cheek.

"That's true," both ladies responded.

"I'm sorry if I don't tell you that enough," Elijah continued. "I just get caught up in this work, and…"

"S'all good," Juliette responded. "You needn't apologize," silencing him with a kiss.

"I'm going to give you lovebirds a bit of space," Moneypenny stated, starting to get up from her seat.

"Mmmmmmmm," said Elijah, breaking free (momentarily) from Juliette's kiss. "Actually, Moneypenny, could you ask Dustin and Harjit to come and see me, please?"

"Of course," Moneypenney replied, moving to the front of the bus. Elijah threw a blanket over Juliette and began to tickle her. She tried to stay still, but Elijah was a pretty good tickler. "Resistance is futile," he whispered to his fiancée.

"Ahem. Sorry to interrupt, but Moneypenny said you wanted to see us?"

"Yeah, thanks," Elijah said slipping from boyfriend into PM mode. "Have you had a chance to read the latest Briefing Notes?"

"We have indeed," Dustin Trudel replied.

"We suspect that you want to discuss the United Nations meeting?" Harjit Singh added.

"Absolutely. I think we three should attend and have Harjit present his proposal to the General Assembly…, but let's have Harjit present to this crowd first."

Elijah went to the front of the Magic Bus, and asked Danni to pull over. When the bus stopped moving, he addressed the ministers through the microphone. "Hey, you crazy kids. We're gonna chill here for a few minutes. Dustin, Harjit and myself are going to attend an emergency UN meeting tomorrow in Geneva. I'd like you to listen to Harjit's proposal that he'll give to the Security Council. As always, please wear your devil's advocate hats and let's use any questions or constructive criticism that you have to improve our proposal."

The United Nations had hastily relocated to Geneva from New York when the Resistance Rallies started and President Trimp declared martial law. They were using the old League of Nations palatial buildings "until the situation in the USA stabilizes," the secretary-general stated in a press release.

After 90 minutes of heated debate, a car came to pick up Elijah, Dustin Trudel and Harjit Singh. The car sped off towards Ottawa.

Lac Champlain, Quebec

A few moments later Danni Grey Eyes wheeled the Magic Bus off the highway, where a waiting crew of people were eager to show off the merits of a solar road.

"As you can see, it's minus 11 here today. Last night we had 16 centimetres of snow that fell on the traditional road beside it. You can see the difference—the solar road is bare and clear of snow."

"The electrical power captured by the solar panels can be used two ways," a young scientist was explaining excitedly to the group. "First, the panels can store and generate heat to keep the road clear when there is snow or freezing rain falling. But snow and freezing rain only fall 3.5 per cent of the year, so when the road is clear, the power can be redirected to the electrical grid."

The Magic Bus crew was impressed, but also had a million questions. "What's the cost to build one kilometre of this solar road, four lanes wide?" Less asked as finance minister. "Well, Sir, currently it's twenty million dollars per kilometre, but with economies of scale, we believe we could lower that to nine or ten million dollars per kilometre," the developer responded. "And what is the cost of one kilometre of standard road, four lanes wide?" Less continued. "It's about 1.1 million dollars to build a standard road," the young man replied. "But..."

"I was hoping there'd be a 'but,'" Less joked.

"The standard road ends up costing the same ten million dollars per kilometre over a 20-year lifespan, when we factor in cost of maintenance and labour for salting, sanding and ploughing the road during the winter."

His associate excitedly jumped into the discussion again. "Here's the better part: the solar road starts to look much cheaper over a 20-year cycle when we factor in the electricity it delivers to the grid. We have estimated that 1,000 kilometres of solar road could deliver 10,000 megawatt hours of electricity per year..."

"That's enough electrical energy to sustain a city of one million people for one year," a third partner chimed in.

Less was frantically punching numbers into a calculator, while the first developer picked it up the topic. "Another easier way to explain the cost benefit analysis is like this," he stated, writing quickly on a whiteboard. "Every kilometre of solar road generates enough electrical power to support 100 homes, or 250 people. Canada has one million kilometres of roads, so we could theoretically support 100 million homes, or 250 million people, with power." The solar road developers were on a roll now, eyes blazing. The second that one of the managers stopped to catch their breath, another started.

"But we only have 38 million people living in Canada, so the excess power could be sold, or used to support winter greenhouses, which could further lower our carbon footprint by reducing food imports…"

"The roads could also easily generate enough power to fuel electric cars, further lowering our use of carbon-based fuels…"

"And, of course, the power could be used to heat all our homes and buildings with renewable electricity, again, further reducing our consumption of oil, firewood and natural gas massively…"

"And the electrical grid, plus all the communication wires currently strung up on poles, can be built into the road, negating the need for poles, which saves even more money and reduces electrical outages during wind and freezing rain events…"

"These guys are like the coolest nerds ever," Danni whispered to Juliette. "I know," whispered Juliette. "If the prime minister hadn't just recently impregnated me, then asked me to marry him on live TV, I'd be all over Nerd Number Two."

"The blond nerd?" Danni asked.

"Hmm, he's cute too, but the Japanese nerd! OMG… he could quantum my physics any day!" Juliette whispered back, as the girls took a giggle fit.

"Isn't a solar road slippery?" Charley was asking. "I mean, this is glass, right?"

"It is glass, but we fabricate it to be rough and pebbly. Just feel it for yourself."

Charley and the rest of the ministers were now on their hands and knees, surprised at how rough the road felt.

"We've been running some tests on the road with different tires," Scientist Number Two was explaining. "The best tire we have found for the solar road is made of softer rubber. It ensures the best traction during steering and for stopping power."

"What about a solar roof?" Charley asked, walking towards the demo model. "Aren't the roof panels easier to build and install? Wouldn't they last longer without vehicles driving on them? I mean, the road idea seems terrific, but I'm concerned about its durability and the return on investment. A roof with interconnected solar shingles tied into the grid? To my simple mind that just seems more achievable."

Before the solar scientists could respond, Less jumped in with more thoughts. "Yeah, I have the same concerns as Charley. It might be hard to design panels tough enough for roads. Instead, we could offer homeowners a subsidized new solar roof if they agree to put their excess power into the grid."

Less was on a roll, thinking out loud. "The building owner gets a new roof at low cost, plus enough free power to sustain a household. With an average house, would there be any power left over to put into the grid?"

"The short answer is yes. There will be power left over from a regular household's use. Obviously, the amount of photovoltaic power generated from a roof or a road depends on a few factors, but primarily it depends on how much sun is shining on the solar collectors. Thunder Bay and Edmonton get more clear, sunny days than Victoria and St. John's. But in either case, the ROI is very good." The scientists held up a hefty-looking file. "We have prepared a package for you that lays out the business case for either project." The file looked pretty ominous. "Or we can give you an e-copy if you prefer? A show of hands, please?"

Most of the ministers quickly raised their hands and nodded. Charley and Less were the last two who reluctantly put their hands up, when Elizabeth Day glared at them.

"E-files for everyone, always," the environment minister said sternly.

The visit ended on optimistic notes with promises of further funding for more research, development and implementation.

Niagara Falls Armory, Ontario

"One Platoon, att-ent-ion!"

The new recruits were doing their best, but their very best wasn't very good, according to their drill instructor, the recently promoted Cpl. Lumpy Halerewich. He was currently providing them with guidance and encouragement in the fashion that drill instructors have used for millennia. His voice was crisp, loud and it cut like a knife.

"In a moment, I will dismiss you. Not now, you horrible little man. Fall back in the ranks and wait for my word of command!" Lumpy shrieked. The young man who had dared to move was turning an unusual shade of crimson.

"You do not deserve to be dismissed. If it were up to me, we would do this all day. However, regulations require that I give you a five-minute break from drill every two hours. Therefore, when you are dismissed you will take a break for five minutes so that you slack and idle individuals can sort yourselves out. I strongly suggest that you hydrate during this break. When we fall in again, your efforts on this parade square will be more energetic, precise and intense. Your movements will be quick and sharp. If I do not see you as one cohesive unit drilling together with drive and energy, we will drill here all night. Is that clear?" Lumpy shouted.

"Yes, Corporal," the new recruits answered raggedly.

"Turning right, dis-missed!" Lumpy barked at the newest members of Canada's militia. The group was supposed to execute a crisp right turn, pause, two, three, then march off smartly. That didn't happen. Of course, it never happened on the first day.

"Corporal Halerewich!" Sgt-Maj. Lee was calling him.

Lumpy marched over smartly and halted crisply one metre in front of the sergeant major.

"Stand at ease. Stand easy. Walk with me, Corporal." Sgt-Maj. Lee had been a militia member for 12 years. She was the consummate professional soldier and strove to pass along her knowledge at every opportunity.

"Corporal, you are aware that my husband is a member of this unit as well, yes?"

"Yes, Sergeant Major."

"You may have also noticed that we keep our distance from each other in a professional sense while at this unit, yes? Even though I outrank my husband, I am careful never to allow myself to be seen as being in a direct line of supervision over my spouse. The reason for this is simple: If my husband were to be treated favourably by me and promoted, or given the pick of duties and responsibilities, other soldiers could view this as favouritism or nepotism. Do you see where I'm going with this, Corporal?"

"Sergeant Major, is this about Recruit Gonzalez?" Lumpy asked nervously. "I mean, we're not official, or…"

"Of course, it's about the young lady, you lummox," Sgt.-Maj. Lee responded good naturedly. "Look, you're not in trouble, this is just some advice from someone who has seen friendship turn to hen shit over simple issues like working together. Within one day, all the recruits in her platoon are gonna know that you are her boyfriend. And that will get tongues wagging. 'He treats her better than us' or 'What a dick wad. He treats her like shit. I can't believe they're going out.' Either way, that can be hard on both of you. So, there is a simple solution. I already explained it to Corporal Brown. He'll take over One Platoon, and you take over Two Platoon. Understood?"

"Yes, Sergeant Major." Lumpy hesitated, then asked, "Sergeant Major Lee, how did you know that Gonzalez and I were a…thing?"

"*Abuela* Rosa told me at church. They were all so proud at their citizenship ceremony, and Rosa is over the moon that Fabiola and Valariano are able to join the militia. They are a lovely family, and she seems like a wonderful young lady." Sgt.-Maj. Lee checked her watch. "Those recruits aren't gonna drill themselves, Halerewich. You're dismissed."

Lumpy snapped to attention, executed an about turn and marched smartly back to the parade square. With a voice like a cracking whip, Cpl. Lumpy Halerewich ordered the ragtag collection of humans now known collectively as Two Platoon to "Fall in!"

"Lumpy, do the corporals always yell at the new soldiers like today?" Fabiola asked as they walked back to Gramma Hanna's.

"Only for a few weeks, *chica*, then we gradually relax as the new soldiers learn what they need to do." They walked silently for a minute. "Why? Did you like it?" Lumpy asked hopefully.

"*Si*. After I learn all the words, I wanna yell at you like that. Wouldn't that be fun?" Fabiola asked mischievously.

"Yes, it would be fun. Just not in public though, OK?"

"It'll be our little secret, *chico*."

Maple Ridge, British Columbia

"We have had six really good sessions with Susanna," a child psychologist was telling KT. "She is a lovely, bright, caring child. We know that she suffered some horrible abuse from infancy until the age of four. Susanna seems to have blocked out that abuse. If she remembers it, she isn't telling us, even under hypnosis. She has wonderful, happy memories of her time in SimpleTown, however. But she seems to have blocked out any memory of her birth parents' recent visit."

KT shuddered at the thought of that event. She had not been sleeping well and had asked for treatment. *I stomped a human being to death* is what she bolted awake thinking at 3 a.m. every morning.

"KT, what you went through that day was extremely shocking. It's perfectly normal to be traumatized by something that horrific."

"I'm more concerned for Susanna's health than my own," KT said. "She suffered through four years of abuse. Then just when she must have thought she was safe, her abusers returned. For me it was a five-minute trip into hell. Can she really be all right?"

"KT, the human brain is still a big mystery. One possible thing working in Susanna's favour is likely her age. A lot of doctors believe that young people can suppress and block out trauma more effectively than adults can, and then carry on as if nothing had happened." The doctor consulted her notes. "You asked last week about putting Susanna into the public-school system. We suggest it's a great idea, but we also recommend a slow start. Maybe mornings only three times a week, then slowly let her grow into it? You've been homeschooling her with the two Mahmoud children, yes?"

"OK, let me think about it," KT replied. *I'm afraid to let her go,* the voices in her head whispered.

"Now for you. Did you want to continue with a mild sedative at night to help you sleep? Or we can increase or lower the dose slightly?"

"I'd like to try for a week without the medication at all," KT replied, feeling optimistic.

"How about a compromise?" the doctor asked, smiling. "I know you said the sedative makes you feel drowsy and groggy. What if I cut the dose in half? You can try to sleep without it, and if you need to take one or two in order to sleep, then you'll have them."

"I can live with that," KT said.

"And look, here is Miss Susanna," said a second doctor. The doctor and Susanna came out looking like happy chipmunks with bulging cheeks. They were both wearing big smiles and giggling.

"Same time next week?"

"You bet," said KT.

Susanna high fived both doctors silently. It was hard to talk with that much special doctor candy in your mouth.

"Let me control the media and I will turn any nation into a herd of pigs."
—Nazi Propaganda Minister Joseph Goebbels

CHAPTER 10

Control the Media, Control the Message

Washington DC

"Here's the plan going forward," Trimp outlined confidently to his small team of confidants. "And it's a terrific plan. Right, Mike?"

"The best plan ever, Mr. President!" Mike Pens boomed emphatically.

"We are going to put out several press releases from the White House," Trimp continued. "Sarah has included those releases in your briefing notes."

Sarah Huckleberry Slanders had proved her worth over the years to Mr. Trimp as the White House press secretary, and Trimp saw no need to replace her. She was a loyal and faithful servant who would ultimately follow the money and power.

"I'll give you all a few minutes to read these pending releases." Trimp paced the room while Sarah passed out the files and the group began scanning the releases.

IVANKA TRIMP NAMED SECRETARY OF STATE: President Trimp announced his new Secretary of State today: Ivanka Trimp. "Many Americans, I mean, really, almost all Americans —except the haters, losers and traitors—have been demanding that I appoint Ivanka Trimp as Secretary of State. She is, without question, the most qualified—far more than Crooked Mallory—the most qualified person ever to fill this position. And she'll be the best, just the best ever. Trust me."

RESISTANCE RALLIES LOSING MOMENTUM: President Trimp today encouraged Americans to return to work and go back to school. "Those traitors arrested at Resistance Rallies are now realizing that their actions were short-sighted, unAmerican, reckless and dangerous. Michelle Oobima agrees with me," said President Trimp, "And Michelle Oobima is encouraging Independent politicians to withdraw their nomination from the upcoming election in November."

AMERICA, MEET YOUR NEW JOINT CHIEFS!: America's four Joint Chiefs of Staff have simultaneously resigned. "It's time for new blood and a new direction," stated Admiral McHale. "We have full confidence that President Trimp's new Joint Chief selections will bring new vitality and energy to these important positions."

INDEPENDENT PARTY DECLARED UNCONSTITUTIONAL: Supreme Court Justice Bart Kavanaugh, a Constitutional expert, ruled today that "the Independent Party has no Constitutional merit, and that Independents could not legally form a government in accordance with the sacred documents our Founding Fathers wrote before God."

PEOPLE'S MILITIA TO THE RESCUE: In a show of true American patriotism, numerous People's Militia groups across the USA are offering their services to President Trimp to quell the illegal and unAmerican "Resistance Rallies."

"I'm proud to accept the service of these highly respected American militia groups," President Trimp said proudly. "The Oath Keepers, Arizona Border Recon, The Three Percenters, Michigan Milita, Hutarees, Tennessee Freedom Fighters, Texas Light Foot Militia, Fraternal Order of the Alt Knights. Idaho Light Militia, Ohio Defense Force, Missouri Militia, Montana Mountain Men, Pennsylvania Military Reserve, New York Light Foot Militia, Green Mountain Boys, Christians for the Constitution—these patriotic Americans represent the very best of our country."

"OK, I can see you've all read the press releases," Trimp continued enthusiastically. "We will have Sarah release this news in about 30 minutes. Following these releases, well, you tell them Ivanka, it was your idea. And it's a great idea. Just terrific."

"Thanks, Daddy," Ivanka giggled happily. "Right now, there are too many bad people saying lies and Fake News about Daddy on the internet. So, we'll have our friends in the new 'Space Force' adjust our satellites enough to temporarily disable the internet, cellular service, social media platforms, and most television and radio stations."

The newly appointed chief of the Space Force nodded his assent.

"We'll blame this 'attack' on 'L'il Rocket Man,'" continued Ivanka excitedly. "Everyone knows he's crazy and doesn't love America the way he should. We will also tell the public that we apprehended these evil doers in the act of damaging our satellites. However, not all our satellites were damaged, and that the Fox satellites are still functional. Like this, we can continue to 'control' the message and the media—just for a few days. Also, our government site—the intranet—will still be functional, allowing our government to communicate and function normally." Ivanka concluded her plan with a curtsy and a giggle.

"Just wonderful, sweetie. Brilliant," her father opined proudly, clapping enthusiastically.

"It hurts me to do this," he continued, arms out like a Mississippi tent revival preacher, as if it really did cause him pain. "Because I truly believe in the First Amendment and freedom of speech with all my heart, but there are evil people in our country. Crazy Michelle Oobima, and Crooked Mallory, and all the Fake News media people, are spreading lies and trying to do great harm to the freedom and democracy we enjoy in America. And it's the best freedom, really, just the greatest. Once we stabilize this great nation and silence the leadership of the Independent Party, we can return to normal. Questions? Yes?"

"Mr. President?" the new director of Homeland Security/Team America was wondering: "These militia groups? Are they reporting to me and my department? And if so, what is their intended role?"

"Mike?"

While Pens outlined his plan for Command and Control with Team America, Trimp practised his putting on a green he had installed a few weeks back. The hole was larger than normal, and the floor bowed towards the hole from all angles imperceptibly. It was difficult for him miss to a putt on this green.

And the crowd around the 18th green at the Masters rises as one to pay homage to the amazing Donald Trimp the sports announcer who rented space in Donald Trimp's head was saying. He snapped out of his golf-induced trance. Ivanka was tugging at his sleeve.

"Daddy, we're wondering if the meeting is over?"

"We interrupt our regularly scheduled Fox programming with this breaking news," Shawn Hanratty said. "The CIA has apprehended North Korean agents who hacked into and disabled multiple American satellites. The North Korean saboteurs disabled approximately 80 per cent of America's satellites before being apprehended by our agents…"

The instant economic effect of no internet service was widespread. The shutdown instantly crippled banks, stock markets and online trading sites such as Amazon and eBay. Major chain stores could not scan bar codes, record sales transactions, or accept credit or debit payment. There simply was no backup system. Many companies had always thought about building in a backup system that would allow them to remain open in the event of an internet shutdown, but very few companies had put that thought into action. Previous internet outages had only lasted several hours, a day at most. "We'll treat it like a long weekend or snow day," most CEOs announced. "If it crashes, close the doors and send the employees home."

On this particular day, as per their standard operating procedures, banks closed instantly when the internet crashed. Bank mangers tried to explain to customers that "the bank needs internet service in order to operate. We want to help you, but we can't." Mobs who wanted to withdraw money howled outside their doors and smashed their way in through windows only to find locked safes. Money machines aka automatic tellers weren't working. Stock brokers were unable to sell stocks from panicked customers because there was no backup system.

Large companies that kept their inventory on the road and relied on "just in time" delivery had no way of ordering stock. Inventory (for the past 10 or 20 years) had been counted by a scanner that read barcodes and ordered more product automatically when the stock level was at 10 or 20 per cent. Very few employees remembered how to do a manual stocktaking. Even if they did physically count the inventory, shipping companies had no way to receive the orders without the internet.

Universities closed, as did most schools. Hospitals and clinics could only offer emergency services and had to reschedule complex operations. Planes, trains and automobiles still worked, but not the Global Positioning Satellite systems in them.

Smaller companies and more agile or adaptable businesses—independent corner stores, small restaurants, food trucks, etc.—were doing brisk business, especially in smaller towns or neighborhoods where people still knew and trusted each other.

"Mr. Hooper, my momma sent me with this grocery list, but she can't get any cash."

"You tell your momma we'll figure it out when this interweb business gets fixed. For now, you get what you need, and I'll write it in this here book," the Mr. Hoopers of America responded.

Landlines were working for those rare people who still had a home or office phone, as were fax machines. "How the @#$% does that work?" the few people still trying to function in an office wondered.

Twitter, Instagram, Facebook, Google, YouTube and the like were all down. In 2018, a Gallup Poll revealed that more than 70 per cent of Americans spent at least two hours a day receiving information, searching for information, or communicating via these social media platforms. The same poll revealed that the same 70 per cent of Americans got their news this way, rather than from traditional news broadcasts or newspapers.

Katy Parry, Justine Bieber and Barrack Oobima were Twitter's top three most-followed people in North America, each having more than 100 million followers. Even if people over 25 considered the first two to be lightweights, when they shared an opinion on Twitter, it got re-tweeted by those followers, exponentially multiplying the people who read it. In case you were wondering: none of these three people would consider themselves conservatives.

Rihanno, Taylor Clift and Eileen DeGeneres were the number four, five and six most-followed persons in the Twittersphere. Again, some people might call them intellectual lightweights, or laugh them off as celebrities. "They aren't real people. They're a managed brand." Nevertheless, when they had an opinion, it got read and then shared a gazillion times by their followers. It's safe to say that these people were outspoken critics of any Republican Party policies of the past 10 years, and especially of Mr. Trimp.

From number seven to 19 in Twitter popularity were a whole bunch of entertainers, plus CNN News and a cute soccer player from Portugal. Still, not a single voice supporting the right side of any political spectrum.

At number 20 stood the most controversial tweeter in the platform's short history. @realdonaldtrimp had almost 50 million followers. (Note: 20 million of those followers were Russian 'bots,' nevertheless, Trimp counted them as loyal followers.) Now, don't forget, Mr. Trimp shared some incredible similarities with the 19 people ahead of him on the list. He was first, foremost and always a showman, an entertainer, the chief ring master of the amazing, baffling circus that was Trimp Inc. Donald J. Trimp was like the evil villain in wrestling. In fact, he had wrestled on some occasions to promote the Trimp brand. People followed and watched Trimp because he was a human train-wreck. It was impossible to look away. Make no mistake, Donald J. Trimp was a brand, and by extension, so were his offspring. The Trimp brand stood for money and power and having the best of everything. If you didn't have those things, then you were quite simply, a loser.

Donald J. Trimp had never told the truth. Ever. Never ever. He was a serial cheat and liar who started with a fortune and turned it into a slightly bigger fortune by conning millions of customers, then declaring bankruptcy, leaving suppliers and customers on the hook (while the Trimp company had made millions.) He had some very good (crooked) tax accountants, and some very good (filthy, dirty, gutter-dwelling, unscrupulous) lawyers.

In his bestselling book *The Art of The Steal*, he outlined (for $29.99) the simple Trimp formula to earn money and acquire power. (The entire philosophy could be captured on one page):

"You want money and power? Then remember this. Every minute, every day, in everything you do. You are never wrong. You are the Boss. What you are selling is unquestionably the very best ever. Fire those subordinates who question your direction. Fire them publicly and damage their reputations as they leave humiliated. Someone hits out, you hit back! Ten times harder, with 10 times more, bigger, better, nastier lawyers. You are never wrong. Lie. Repeat the lie. Have your subordinates repeat it. Repeat it again and again and again. Now they believe you. You are the Boss. You grab what you want, when you want it. You don't ask, you grab! What you are selling is unquestionably the very best ever. Money. Girls. Power. Just grab. You are the Boss. You are never wrong. Grab it!"

Surprisingly, Trimp wrote six other books with different titles (but remarkably similar advice) that all sold reasonably well to the type of people who dreamed about living the Trimp lifestyle.

Trimp hotels, restaurants, casinos, condos, vacation properties and golf courses were dreadfully garish, hideously tacky and vastly overpriced. But to the welder from Woonsocket, or the machinist from Monterry, one night in a Trimp hotel with the missus (or mistress) was like a dream come true. *Such opulence! Such grandeur! A solid gold toilet! Everything was the biggest and best!*

Maybe a Trimp tie fits your budget better? "These are the best ties ever made."

Or some highly sought-after shoes from Ivanka's line of Trimp footwear. "These shoes are the best. No shoes have ever been better."

A flight on Trimp Air? "The world's greatest airline."

Or perhaps a Trimp Steak, "cut by the very best butchers from the very best and biggest cattle in America, served with the world's best red wine: a Trimp Cabernet."

How about a degree from Trimp University? "Only the best and brightest study and teach here."

So, given his history of consistently lying about everything, and his consistent history of being a hideous, pussy-grabbing racist, bully and conman, approximately 70 per cent of the people who followed @realdonaldtrimp on Twitter followed him out of hate and/or morbid curiosity. Trimp would tweet a lie from his gold toilet at Mar-a-Lago at 0300, and within 24 hours, 10,000 people would comment on his lie, and provide the actual facts/point out the lie/accuse Trimp of being a hideous hateful monster/point out his many other character flaws/accuse him of criminal activity/tell the public in the Twittersphere that they pray nightly for his death, imprisonment or impeachment.

The other 30 per cent of Trimp's Twitter followers—the bots and Trimpanzees—would re-tweet their hero's message, and comment in a supportive way, normally suggesting that God or Republican Jesus would bless Mr. Trimp for MAGA! Often, in the same thread of the tweet, the Trimp lovers would then argue with Trimp haters, eventually calling each other "uneducated trailer trash, inbred racist hillbilly, illiterate deplorable," and so on.

Some possible responses to those slurs included "unemployed snowflake, faggot, triggered spoon-fed millennial…" By simply reading his Twitter history, it was easy to surmise that the mere mention of Trimp had a massively divisive effect.

And Trimp was a serial Tweeter. Like a bloated, pugnacious bully, he lashed out at enemies via Twitter from his golden throne, often giving his enemies schoolyard nicknames. "L'il Rocket Man," "Pocahontas," "Crooked Mallory," "Sloppy Steve," "Cryin' Chuck," and so many more. The function of these tweets was twofold: promote his idea or brand while simultaneously ridiculing those who opposed him.

As these social media platforms became more popular in the twentyteens, people chose online friends who reflected their own personal views. Since most people were getting their news via social media, the American people and their media operated in two pipelines or silos that delivered news from a left or right perspective. The only time a liberal would quote a Republican would be to accuse them of lying for personal or political gain, and vice versa.

The name or brand of Trimp was now officially a social hand grenade. Try it yourself. Announce in a room full of people that you are or were a staunch Trimp supporter. Now watch the room divide. Depending on your location, (Alabama or California?) between 50 to 98 per cent of the room will step away as if you are leprous and your sores are open and oozing. Note: The experiment doesn't work as well the other way around. Denounce Trimp in any

"People are really stupid."

Thankfully, not all the American people were as stupid as Mr. Trimp wanted to believe. Despite not having the internet, and Fox News being the only available TV station, people were seeing through this ruse and discovering the truth. Newspaper sales were exploding.

Simultaneously, plenty of people printed their own old-school pamphlets or handbills, and were posting them up on phone poles from Nome to Key West, from Baltimore, to Berkeley, and all points in between:

MICHELLE OOBIMA IN PRISON: SHE SAYS DON"T GIVE UP! The accompanying photo showed a badly bruised but defiant-looking Michelle behind bars, flashing a peace sign. "Don't give up," the fiery Independent told us today. "Keep rallying, keep fighting for your freedom. Trimp's government is criminally corrupt, and cannot maintain this level of oppression on the American people."

A similar message was repeated by numerous famous Independent candidates imprisoned in various States. Barney was in jail in Vermont. Jesus Ventura was locked up in Minnesota. Half of Hollywood's celebrities were in prison, including hopeful Independent candidates Dwain John-Stone, Arnold Schwarzenegro, Chelsea Chandler, Sarah Silverstein, Trevor Noa and a whole bunch of their friends.

manner of your choosing, and you will like[ly make]
new friends. Depending on your Trimp posit[ion, you]
make or lose your friends quickly. There is n[o sitting on]
the fence for Trimp. Now expand the room, c[ity by city,]
state by state, county by county. The city, state [and country]
will divide much as the room did.

So, by shutting down the internet, President Tr[imp was]
essentially silencing the hundreds of millions of left-[leaning,]
Trimp-hating dissenting voices that would otherwi[se have]
been communicating via Twitter, Facebook and Insta[gram.]

Leaving Fox as the only functioning TV station wa[s]
diabolically clever. Fox had pulled all its other programn[ing]
and was now a 24-hour entertainment channel pretend[ing]
to be a news channel. Fox and friends relentlessly repeat[ed]
whatever news Trimp, Pens or Sarah Slanders sent the[m]
via the White House communications team.

RESISTANCE RALLIES LOSING MOMENTUM

INDEPENDENT PARTY DECLARED UNCONSTITUTIONAL

PEOPLE'S MILITIA TO THE RESCUE

MICHELLE OOBIMA RESIGNS, TELLS INDEPENDENTS TO STAND DOWN

And so on.

Remember Trimp's advice to those wishing to seize power?

"Tell a lie that supports you or your brand. Make it big. Tell it confidently. Say it loudly and proudly. Lash out at those who dare to disagree and humiliate them. Tell the lie again, and again, and again, and again. For most people, they only need to hear it three times, and they'll believe it," Trimp famously said.

PRESIDENT TRIMP DISABLED INTERNET–KEEP RALLYING–KEEP RESISTING, shouted another handbill.

"According to a United States Cyber Consequences Unit spokesperson, the United States government adjusted American satellites slightly to disrupt internet and television coverage. "It's really quite simple–all these satellites were turned approximately .05 of one degree. That's enough to disrupt service like we are experiencing now. We traced the signal that turned these satellites back to NORAD. Our own government disabled the internet to suppress and control the media."

With many of the Resistance Rally leaders already imprisoned, normal American citizens took up the cause. They printed handbills and posters, the passed the news by word of mouth:

RESISTANCE RALLY TODAY AT NOON–BANGOR, AUGUSTA, PORTLAND, BREWER, LEWISTON, LOS ANGELES, LA JOLLA, SAN DIEGO, SAN FRANCISCO, SANTA CRUZ, BAKERSFIELD…

Small-town mayors and grandmothers were rallying. Principals and teachers took entire classes and entire schools to rallies. Senior citizens in wheelchairs requested volunteers to take them to rallies. Farmers and truckers drove their tractors and 18-wheelers to the rallies. Motor cycle clubs, including the Hells Angels, Satan's Sons and the Blue Knights, were at the rallies.

Fox News tried to deny that the rallies were ongoing, instead mentioning that "Independent leader Michelle Oobima again encouraged people to 'go home, return to work and return to school.'"

President Trimp's Administration was having a hard time getting his foot soldiers to do his bidding. Most peace officers, including Homeland Security personnel and members of the military, were simply refusing Trimp's orders to arrest any more people, and instead, were joining in the rallies to support and protect The Resistance. The protection was important, as many of the People's Militia groups previously mentioned were now zealously trying to arrest or disperse as many "hippies, snowflakes and peaceniks" as possible.

Many of the members of these militia groups were folks who had wanted to join their own regular military or police forces but were found unsuitable during the application process. Most were unable to meet the threshold required on the aptitude or physical fitness test, or had prior criminal history, or were deemed too mentally unstable even for national service. So, a lot of these folks were hoping to finally live their dream and get to do some ass kicking. They normally stood down when confronted by regular police officers, actual military members, or Miss Black's class of third graders.

By the third afternoon of the Resistance Rallies, there were some major problems in the USA. In the 2016 American election, 129 million people voted. The other 127 million eligible voters hadn't bothered to exercise that right. "Why would I vote?" most people responded when asked.

"Really, I get to choose between Mallory Clifton or Donald Trimp? Get outta heah. I don't trust either one. Republican, Democrat—don't matter, nothin' changes."

So, in 2020, there were more people protesting for the right to vote for Independent politicians (by most estimates 140 million people) than had voted in the last election.

Over the three days of Resistance Rallies, 2.7 million Americans had been arrested for unlawful assembly. That number included 13 senators (eight Democrats, four Republicans and one Independent) and 46 Congressmen (23 from each party).

Half a million more Americans were still in Canada, where they had fled to stay warm during the Great Canadian Blackout. Farmers were still farming (if they had livestock to feed), but they were at the rallies in spirit. The only other people still working were those who realized they were essential services. Police, the military, nurses and doctors, snowplough drivers, the guys at your local sanitation department and water treatment plants, the folks who ran generating stations. Newspapers were reporting that 95 per cent of Americans supported having Independent politicians on the ballots.

WHERE IS OUR GOVERNMENT? was the headline in *The New York Times*.

AMERICA? asked *The Guardian* of London.

*The thermophilic composting of human feces and urine (don't call it waste-it has value) requires no electricity and therefore no coal combustion, no acid rain, no nuclear power plants, no nuclear waste, no petrochemicals and no consumption of fossil fuels. The composting process produces no waste, no pollutants and no toxic by-products. Thermophilic composting of humanure can be carried out century after century, millennium after millennium, with no stress on our ecosystems, no unnecessary consumption of resources and no garbage or sludge for our landfills. And all the while it will produce a valuable resource necessary for our survival while preventing the accumulation of dangerous pathogenic waste.
– Joseph Jenkins,* The Humanure Handbook: A Guide to Composting Human Manure

CHAPTER 11

The Shittiest Chapter

Saint-Louis-du-Ha-Ha, Quebec

Charley, having insisted it was his turn to drive, was driving the Magic Bus to its next stop. "We are just a few minutes away from our next visit," he said into the microphone that the driver could use to address (or entertain) the passengers. He had been telling corny jokes and stories for the past 20 minutes. "Less, Elizabeth and I asked for this visit to be added to the list," he cackled in to the mike. "It's so beautifully simple, even I can understand it. You young people are gonna love this project."

Juliette and Danni looked at each other grimly. "Whenever he says stuff like that, I usually think I'm not gonna like it at all," Juliette said quietly.

"I heard that, girlfriend," Charley sang into the mike. Juliette and Danni giggled. Charley wheeled the Magic Bus into a parking lot, with a meadow filled with grazing goats behind it in the distance. A very large lumberjack was waiting for them, leaning on a pitchfork. He remained stone still, like a statue, as the ministers were getting off the bus. The crew all disembarked from the MagicBus and were staring at the lumberjack statue. As Juliette reached out to touch him and see if he was real, he grabbed her hand. She shrieked. He kissed her hand. She blushed. And the lumberjack released her hand gallantly.

"Welcome, friends. Welcome. Together, we are going to learn how to do wonderful things with shit. Hello, *Bonjour*. My name is Gaston LaCroix." Gaston bowed low with a sweeping flourish. "But people also call me Captain CaCa, the Sultan of Shit, the Prince of Piss, and many other flattering things."

Gaston was a very large and very happy man. He looked like the cartoon image of a French-Canadian lumberjack: black toque, wild head of curly black hair, massive black beard, red and black lumberjack shirt, suspenders. The ministers were still giggling at his animated introduction.

"So, the by-product of human digestion shouldn't be called 'human waste' at all. Instead, we need to use the by-product of human digestion as a valuable resource," Gaston was saying.

Most of the ministers looked skeptical, a few even looked grossed out. Gaston was used to seeing that look on people's faces. "All right, let's break it down in simple terms. We all eat, yes?" The ministers nodded and murmured in agreement. Gaston was a bit like a stand-up comic: you wanted to stay engaged in the show, or he might pull you up out of the audience and use you in his skit.

"And we all drink, yes?" Once again, the group dutifully nodded their assent. "Then our bodies digest those things. We extract the nutrients we need from it, and the rest is what we in the western world call human waste: shit, piss, poop, ca-ca, fecal matter. We all shit. We all piss. If we don't, we die! So, let's not be embarrassed by discussing where it goes after we pass it, yes?" The crowd laughed and nodded.

Gaston was walking as he talked. "Please, everyone come into our classroom." He held open the door of a rustic one-room schoolhouse. The 'chairs' were wooden boxes, with a wooden tank on the back and a regular wooden toilet seat on top. "Now, before you shit—I mean sit—please, lift the lid." The visitors did as instructed, giggling, while Gaston narrated. "What do you see?"

"It's a bucket half full of dirt," Benjamin responded.

"Exactly, it is a dry compost toilet. It's very simple and cheap to build, and easy to use. It's a wooden box with a standard toilet seat over a round hole. There is a bucket under the hole. You pee and poo in this bucket like any other toilet. When you are finished, you sprinkle any organic dry material over top of what you just added to the bucket, yes?" Danni had raised her hand.

"Why the dry material? And what do you use? And where is it?"

"Three great questions, *Mademoiselle. Merci, beaucoup*. First, pee and poo by themselves do normally stink. It's a fact." It was hard not to laugh at Gaston's honest descriptions and animated facial expressions. "If we don't cover it, it smells." He held his nose for a minute.

"But when we do cover it, there is no smell!" he shouted triumphantly, arms raised to the heavens. "Also, the dry material helps later when we compost what it in the bucket. Second, the dry material? It can be almost any loose shredded organic material: loose soil, peat moss, sawdust, fine mulch, shredded paper, pine needles, et cetera. Third, where is it? Lift the lid on the toilet tank." The group did as instructed. "What do you see?"

"It looks like good old-fashioned dirt," Charley said. "Exactly," said Gaston. "The dry material can go in the tank on the back of the toilet. So, I will demonstrate how to poop in the compost toilet. Observe closely while I narrate:

1. "Lift lid (Gaston was a great mime, his version of a man pulling down his pants to poo was classic physical comedy).
2. Do your business (wipe your bum).
3. Sprinkle to cover.
4. Close lid! "All good?"

The ministers were nodding and laughing at Captain CaCa's very animated performance. "Good, pull up a seat and let's discuss. I'm sure you have questions?" Gaston nodded at Juliette. "Yes?"

"Why not just flush it away? Isn't that better?" Juliette was blushing but pressed on, like a trooper. "I mean, honestly, pardon my language, but I don't want a pail full of smelly poop in my bathroom while I'm brushing my teeth or having a shower."

Gaston nodded solemnly in agreement. "Yep, I get it. That's a normal reaction to this system from anyone who has always used a flush toilet. But in this room right now there are 30 pails half full of covered crap, in each of your toilets that you are sitting on." The visitors looked awkwardly at each other, some with slight grimaces. "Does anybody smell anything shitty?" Gaston continued, looking around the room, smiling brightly.

The ministers inhaled, trying hard to smell shit but not succeeding. Juliette shifted uncomfortably with the thought she was sitting eight inches above a bucket half filled with poo and pee. Gaston lifted the lid of his toilet seat and put his big bearded lumberjack face almost right in the pail. He inhaled deeply, audibly, came up grinning, and then exhaled. "There is no smell because the poop and pee are covered with the dry material. Do we agree that there is no smell?" The group nodded and murmured their assent. "But I can see that some of you are still not convinced. It's nicer just to flush it away, and have 'it' disappear, yes?"

Half of the room nodded. "You are reading my mind, Captain CaCa," Juliette blushed.

"OK, OK. But let's talk about where 'it' goes when we flush it."

"It just goes away, and after that I don't care about it," Juliette said, with Danni smiling and nodding supportively.

"But where does it go?" Gaston persisted.

"Well, in a city, it goes through a sewer system and into a sewage treatment plant," Benjamin said. "And in rural settings, to a septic tank, which then gets pumped out and hopefully treated in a similar sewage treatment plant."

"Precisely. In some cities and towns, there is a primary sewage treatment plant, built and maintained at tremendous expense. Some cities, like Calgary and Edmonton, have spent billions of dollars on a secondary and tertiary treatment system. And those cities get an A+ for their poop processes." Gaston paused to give a two thumbs up. "But those cities are the exception, not the rule. There are lots of other cities and municipalities all around Canada and the rest of the world that simply flush raw sewage directly into rivers, lakes and harbours. Still more cities have an outdated primary treatment system that often get overwhelmed during heavy rains. When that happens, the raw untreated sewage also ends up in that municipalities rivers, lakes and harbours. Untreated human waste is incredibly dangerous. In Canada our untreated human waste contaminates our watersheds, causing incredible harm to marine life, and polluting our groundwater with heavy metals and disease-carrying bacteria. On a global level, the World Health Organization estimates that two million people each year die from drinking water contaminated by fecal coliform. WHO also estimates that another 10 million people per year die simply from lack of any reliable drinking water at all."

Gaston, thus far had been animated and happy, but now he simply looked disappointed. "Folks, our current system of treating 'human waste' is broken. And it will cost billions of dollars to improve our outdated infrastructure." The ministers did not look optimistic about spending that sort of money on a topic as unsexy as sewage. "But wait," Gaston said. "You haven't heard the worst news about our current traditional waste treatment systems. Even if we spend all that money on upgrading sewage treatment systems, there will still be a fatal, unsustainable flaw. What's the flaw in our current system, even if we throw billions of dollars at it?"

Elizabeth Day, minister of the environment, knew the answer. "We don't have enough fresh water on our planet to sustain global toilet flushing," she replied.

"Nonsense. Canada has 10 per cent of the world's fresh water," Gaston retorted, happily assuming an opposite role.

"We do—for now. Canada has 10 per cent of a rapidly dwindling global supply of fresh water. That doesn't mean we can afford to waste it—16 litres per flush—just to make poop 'go away'" she responded defiantly. "Sixteen litres per flush," she repeated angrily, rising to her feet to face her peers. "So, we have enough water to keep flushing toilets for another 100 years in our country, and then the whole world will be out of fresh water." Gaston was happy to have the leader of the Green Party carrying his torch. He took a seat on one of his eco-toilets while Elizabeth got her green groove on.

"Sixteen litres per flush. Every flush could sustain a family of four over 24 hours. Instead of flushing away our waste, we could save four lives. Our fresh water is a tremendous gift, and we are using it to make shit go away? Worse yet: our 'flushing' system doesn't even work well and is ensuring that human waste is one of the leading pollutants on the planet."

"Well, now I just feel awful," Juliette said. "I'm 'that girl' who just wants the poop to 'go away.'"

"Juliette, we are all 'that girl'," Elizabeth replied kindly, patting her shoulder. Even the men were nodding assent. "The flush toilet was an amazing invention, for its time. But world population has grown 1,000 per cent since its inception, and our planet's water supply is shrinking fast. We need to find a better system—something sustainable." Elizabeth looked around the room with a grin. "We are sitting on the answer."

"*Allons-y!*" cried Gaston, leaping to his feet. "Come with me, my friends. Let's follow this shitty story to a happy ending. I need five brave and fearless volunteers to bring five pails of poop to our laboratory." Five ministers raised their hands and lifted out five pails. Captain CaCa led the group to a series of compost boxes labelled 1, 2, 3, 4…

"Volunteers, one at a time, please empty your poo pails here in box one." Charley, Elizabeth, Benjamin, Danni and Less poured the semi-solid/liquid contents of their buckets into a cubic compost box approximately 1.5 metres on all sides, with an open top.

"It all just looks like moist dirt," Danni said, "with a few pieces of toilet paper here and there. I was honestly expecting something much grosser."

"We are happy to disappoint you in this expectation," Gaston replied cheerfully to Danni. "And now, *Mademoiselle*, would you please just sprinkle on some of this cover material?" Gaston asked Juliette, handing her a shovel from a pile of beautiful, light, loose black compost in box two.

"That's black gold right there, Juliette," Charley said, whistling his appreciation, picking up a handful and squeezing it.

"Indeed, it is, Charley," Gaston nodded, beaming his lumberjack grin. "You are a farmer, yes? And Mr. Izmore as well, I believe?" Both men nodded assent. "Charley, on your farm, what did you do with your shit–I mean your animal shit?"

"Just what you are doing here," Charley replied. "We collect it, cover it with any other organic waste, and let Mother Nature turn it into to this here beautiful black earth. Then we put it back into the earth, work it into a garden, top-dress pasture land, and so forth."

"So, box one is fresh people poop, and box two is the finished product: poop that has just been broken down through aerobic decomposition?" Elizabeth May wondered hopefully.

"Exactly, it's that simple!" the Sultan of Shit shouted joyfully. He repeated:

1. "Empty full pail on pile.
2. Cover pile to block smell.
3. When box is full, let it rest for one year."

"Thermophilic composting kills any diseases we carry. *Et voila*, Mother Nature and her magical bacteria do the rest. The finished product is beautiful nutrient-rich, odour-free black earth. It has value. It is NOT waste. It is incredibly good fertilizer," he added passionately. "Currently, we sell a 50-litre bag of our compost for $3.99, and we can't keep up to the demand from gardeners and small farms. We have set up 750 households and businesses in this community with eco-toilets. We go pick up their shit and turn that shit into money!" Gaston smiled gently, like a giant friendly bear. "Those households save money on their water bill and feel good about helping to reduce pollution. The municipality saves money in lower sewage treatment plant operating costs, and lower usage of city water.

"Oh. I almost forgot to add two important things we can extract from poo and pee. First, in our larger composting operation out back, we are generating electricity from the methane the pile produces as it breaks down. From our pile out back, we generate enough power to run this business, five electric trucks and 15 households. Second, we are finding significant traces of precious metals in our piles of poop: gold, silver, vanadium, aluminum. We did a study last year with funding from the Ministry of Natural Resources. The study indicates that the poop from one million people in one year contains 17 million dollars' worth of precious metals. So, a city the size of Toronto is pooping out 85 million dollars' worth of precious metals that are currently contaminating Lake Ontario." The ministers looked excited by this unexpected news of further value from what was currently considered waste.

"Imagine what a city could do with 85 million dollars," Elizabeth Day added.

Benjamin Big Canoe looked briefly at his watch. "Gaston, I think we all see the benefit of compost toilets. They save water, save money, reduce pollution and turn what we think is waste into a resource, or several valuable resources. I also believe we understand that flush toilets are environmentally unsustainable, massively expensive to maintain and cause pollution. But how do we convince people to switch from flush toilets to dry compost toilets?"

"Especially in cities and apartments," his girlfriend added. "I mean, an apartment dweller can't be expected to build a compost pile."

"Well, the Chinese and Vietnamese people have been doing this in towns and cities for centuries. Apartment dwellers put their covered pails in a space beside the garbage bins. There are 'night soil' companies that drive around much like garbage trucks, pick up full buckets, and drop off empty clean buckets. Those companies then compost everybody's poop and sell the finished product," Gaston replied. "The composting companies could be public or privately owned. Now if you gave people a tax refund for using the composting system, and simultaneously added a significant flush toilet tax, you'd see people make the switch pretty quick," Gaston suggested.

"Public education would also play an important role," Juliette mused. "People wanna do the right thing, but sometimes we aren't even aware that there is a problem. Until today, I didn't even know that flush toilets were causing these problems, or that there was a viable cost-effective alternative."

"It's no different than recycling," the environment minister added. "Thirty years ago, everything went into the trash. Then we educated the public that we couldn't do that, that we needed to Reduce, Re-use and Recycle everything we could. Now we reward people who recycle with refunds and punish those who don't with extra service charges when we pick up their trash."

"Gaston, I'm gonna get our CBC crews to start discussions with you about educational videos. I would suggest a cartoon form for younger audiences, and a more science-based, factual version for audiences over 12 years old," the minister of youth offered enthusiastically.

Amid promises of further communication, 'humanure' how-to instructions, funding for educational commercials, and precious metal extraction research, the ministers were boarding the Magic Bus. Captain CaCa was handing out massive bear hugs and "Thanks For Giving A Shit," bumper stickers.

"Politics is the skilled use of blunt objects."
—Lester B. Pearson, founder of UN peacekeeping,
Nobel Peace Prize winner, Canadian
prime minister 1963-1968.

CHAPTER 12

The Russian Bear Rises

Washington DC and Geneva, Switzerland

Keeping Donald Trimp informed and current on important world events was never easy for Trimp's staff. Despite his own claims of being a "stable genius," there were many, many, many things Trimp didn't understand. But Donald Trimp couldn't admit that he didn't understand the complexities of political relationships in the UN, or his own country's Constitution, or why a stealth plane wasn't invisible to the human eye. Nor could he admit that anyone knew more about any topic than himself. Remember, for example, that he knew more about nuclear weapons and ISIS than all his generals.

Mikki Haley was briefing Trimp on the SecureNet screen from Geneva. After 15 seconds, she could see that Trimp wasn't listening. "Vice President Pens, I think it's important that the President hear this brief."

Trimp hadn't been sleeping well. He was having recurring dreams in which all the women he ever slept with were all tweeting and going on TV and laughing at his small hands and small…

"What is it, Mike?" Trimp snapped back into reality with a gasp. Mike Pens was shaking him by the shoulder.

"Sir, UN Representative Haley says it's important that you hear this."

"Go ahead, Mikki. I'm all ears," Trimp assured his UN representative. Ms. Haley was about to resume her brief, but Trimp continued. "A lot of the staff here have told me I'm a much better listener than Oobima was. I may even the best listener of all time. Remember, Mike, when that guy said that? That guy on Fox? It was probably Hanratty, or…?"

"I sure do, Mr. President," his loyal sidekick replied. *I've never heard anyone say that,* a tiny voice in Mike's head was saying.

Mikki Haley took a deep breath and resumed. "The Security Council is voting on an emergency resolution to deploy 250,000 peacekeepers to the United States, Mr. President," the USA's representative to the UN was saying via SecureNet.

"Why, in the name of God, would the United Nations—which is a failure, by the way—think we need peacekeepers?" Trimp demanded haughtily.

"Sir, I'm in Europe, at the United Nations, where the average civilized and educated person currently thinks America is committing some serious human rights transgressions." Mikki relied tersely. "Also, in case you've forgotten, we have imprisoned two or three million citizens in the past few days for demanding democratic freedoms? And you've declared martial law? Now things are unfolding rapidly here, so let me explain what is being discussed."

The rest of the room braced for shock. No one ever spoke to Donald Trimp in condescending or demeaning tones. Those who did were immediately fired, disgraced, humiliated and dragged through the mud.

Mike Pens knew why she could get away with it, but his Christian family values wouldn't let his inside voice become his outside voice anytime soon. *Shut up, inside voice,* Mike Pens whispered softly to himself.

Representative Haley read from her notes. "The resolution states that the UN 'may deploy peacekeeping forces when it has reasonable cause to believe that:

- a government is actively involved in human rights abuses against its citizens;
- a government's security forces are overwhelmed and conditions for further violence against its citizens by rogue elements are imminent;
- a majority of citizens in a nation state express a lack of confidence in their government and concern that the government is not acting in the best interests of its citizens; and
- there is concern that a government is unfairly tampering with or refusing to allow for a fair and reasonable electoral process.'"

Mikki Haley looked up expectantly for Trimp's response.

Pens whispered in Trimp's ear.

"As one of the five permanent members of the Security Council, we'll simply use our veto power, and the resolution will be quashed," Trimp said confidently. "Quashed. You know, Mikki, a lot of people don't even know that's a real word." Trimp was going to keep babbling about his knowledge of many good and bigly words from his Ivy League education because he went to the best schools, but Mikki Haley pressed on.

"Actually, Mr. President, there is a problem with that assumption," his UN representative was telling him. "When the UN considers deploying peacekeepers into a nation, that country in question is not able to participate in voting on the resolution. A recent example would be Afghanistan. Do you think the UN listened to the Afghanistan government when it said, 'We don't want or need the International Security Assistance Force in our country?'"

"America is not a shithole like Afghanistan. You need to ensure that the UN understands our position," the POTUS stated angrily. He stopped for a moment. "Mike, what is our position on this again?" he whispered quietly.

Mike Pens and an executive assistant had been madly typing in the background, and Pens passed Trimp a note.

Trimp assumed his presidential stance. "This is what they need to hear, Mikki. And I quote—I mean, you quote me. Make sure they know this is my thoughts and writing."

Mikki Haley looked like she was dying slowly.

"America is the most powerful nation on this planet. And has the most freedom, no, the greatest freedom. The USA will not allow UN peacekeepers to enter our country. If the UN deploys peacekeepers to the USA, we will consider that deployment an act of aggression against our nation. Any peacekeepers who enter the USA will be considered as hostile forces and will be killed or captured as prisoners of war. The USA is not a banana republic that requires third-party intervention to ensure a fair electoral process."

Trimp looked up from his notes. "Is that all clear, Representative?"

"Crystal clear, Mr. President," Mikki replied in a cold voice. "The vote is in 20 minutes. I will ensure that the Security Council hears your message before the vote."

"Representative Haley, worst-case scenario?" the new Secretary of State Ivanka Trimp was asking, reading from notes prepared by another nameless assistant. "Even if—for some totally stupid and suicidal reason, cuz nobody should cross daddy, cuz he always wins—the UN decides to deploy peacekeepers to the USA, what's the timeline? Everybody knows—cuz daddy told us—the UN is a hopeless bureaucratic mess. Every peacekeeping nation's troops are already deployed in Africa and similar Third World locations. It'll take six months to even select the troop-contributing nations, and another three months to train them. By the time the UN gets its act together, these ridiculous rallies will be over, and the election will be finished. And daddy will be president for another four years." Ivanka finished on a high note, and hopped up and down, clapping her hands excitedly for emphasis.

There was brief time delay while Representative Haley heard and then registered what the new secretary of state was saying. It would have been obvious to most people that could read body language or interpret facial expressions that Mikki Haley was wondering why she had agreed to take this job during the Trimp Administration.

"Well, normally, Madame Secretary, you'd be right. But these are not normal times. This particular resolution is being sponsored by Elijah and his Canadian government. Their defence minister has significant peacekeeping experience. He has convinced the Security Council that Canada could have 250,000 troops ready to deploy in 36 hours if the resolution is approved."

President Trimp and the rest of his inner circle tensed up noticeably. "Ridiculous and impossible!" Ivanka cried, stomping her foot for emphasis. "Canada has, like, the tiniest military ever."

"Well, Madame Secretary," the chairman of the Joint Chiefs interjected. "The Canadian Armed Forces was indeed very small in the recent past. However, the Canadian government has been conscripting and enlisting new citizen-soldiers at a tremendous rate. Joining the military has become the latest cool trendy thing to do in Canada. Our latest intelligence indicates that the Canadian military now has close to one million personnel."

As Trimp and his secretary of state considered that surprising new information, Mikki Haley was signing off. "The council votes in 15 minutes. I'll present a rebuttal to the resolution and let you know the results ASAP."

The next 30 minutes in the president's briefing room were not pleasant. Trimp had hoped that the Resistance Rallies would have lost momentum by now. The exact opposite was happening.

His advisors were droning on...

The rallies were uniting communities at the grassroots level. There were neighborhood rallies, district rallies, hockey and basketball tournament rallies, senior citizens' rallies, gay rodeo rallies, children's rallies, Texas hold'em rallies and punk bluegrass fusion rallies.

Remote rural areas were having rallies in churches, barns and schools. Cowboys, ranchers, oil workers and members of the Sioux Nation rallied together in solidarity at Standing Rock.

Jews, Muslims, Buddhists, Satan worshippers, Baptists, atheists, agnostics, and the LBGTQ community rallied as brothers and sisters for freedom in towns and cities across America.

Resistance Rallies were also taking place around the world. Sydney, Vancouver, Tokyo, Toronto, London, Moscow, Beirut, Dublin, Cardiff, Edinburgh, Barcelona, Hammerfest, Oslo, Cape Town, Tel Aviv, Amsterdam, Rome, Santiago, Paris, Munich, Manila and many more cities hosted rallies.

There were Resistance Rallies on cruise ships and at scientific outposts at the North and South Poles. The Inuit on Baffin Island hosted a Resistance Rally with all you could eat seal heart and blubber. A group of 30 international climbers put a "Resist" sign at the peak of Mount Everest. The crew of the International Space Station held a rally. One hundred monks at a Shaolin temple vowed not to eat or drink until America had freedom. The Vatican was hosting a nonstop freedom and prayer vigil until peace and freedom was restored to America…

The Joint Chiefs of Staff and Homeland Security were reporting that the vast majority of military members, police and security force members were sympathetic to the cause of The Resistance.

"Are we still arresting these traitors?" Trimp snapped. The briefing room went quiet. "Has everyone forgotten that this country is under martial law? I want all these

'Resistance' losers arrested!" he shouted angrily, pounding the table. The personnel around the table looked embarrassed.

"Mr. President, honestly, there are two main reasons why we can't arrest any more people," the chief of Homeland Security replied, standing as he spoke. "First, our prisons were already full before the Resistance Rallies started last week. Since then, we have arrested 2.6 million American citizens. We have no where to put them, and we can't safely house those people we have arrested already. We cannot feed them, there are no washroom facilities, and people are beginning to die while in custody." Heads around the table were nodding silently in agreement.

"Second, most of our security forces–the National Guard, police forces, the military, et cetera–are refusing orders to arrest any more people. Currently, the only people trying to bust up the rallies or arrest anyone are the various People's Militia groups. Commanders of real, qualified, mentally stable security forces on the ground are simply ensuring that the People's Militia members don't kill resistance members or vice versa."

The room went awkwardly silent. Many of the president's appointees and advisors suddenly became interested in their shoes. Trimp remained strangely calm as he struggled to digest this latest news.

"Daddy," his secretary of state was saying, "the UN lady wants to talk to you again." She nodded at the screen.

Trimp swivelled in his chair to see the screen better. As she stood to address the United Nations Security Council in Geneva, Mikki Haley looked and sounded like a woman on a mission. She spoke proudly, passionately and defiantly, telling the Security Council precisely (minus Trimp's broken thoughts) the message that her president had dictated to her a few moments earlier. The camera panned around the room as she spoke and focused for a minute on the Canadian politicians: Elijah, Harjit Singh and Dustin Trudel. The other UN representatives looked uninterested or unimpressed with what Mikki Haley was saying. When she finished speaking, she took her seat.

No one applauded.

"All in favour of United Nations Resolution 176 B, please rise," the secretary-general was saying. Almost the entire room stood, while UN administrative staff recorded which countries were in favour of the resolution.

"All nations abstaining."

Israel, really? You couldn't be opposed? Representative Haley thought.

"All opposed." No one stood.

Mikki Haley looked furious. *Traitorous backstabbing cowardly f @#& ers. After all we've done for you…*

Then, slowly, and amidst a growing crescendo of jeers, boos and whistles, the representative from Russia stood, with Vladimir Poutine at his side.

"As one of the five permanent members of the Security Council, Russia is using its veto power to defeat the resolution," Vladimir Poutine stated curtly in Russian. He glared around the room defiantly as the representatives and heads of state continued to jeer and whistle. The jeers and catcalls grew louder as Poutine's comments were translated into the other five official UN languages: French, Arabic, Chinese, Spanish and English.

US Representative Mikki Haley, looking relieved, came back on the screen via SecureNet. "Well, that was close," she chirped happily. "I spoke to Poutine privately just before the vote. He understands that this 'Resistance' is just a temporary blip on the radar. He thinks the resolution to send in peacekeepers was designed to embarrass and weaken the United States of America. He told me he plans to call you later today, Mr. President."

"Thank you, Representative Haley. Good job," President Trimp said. "Just the greatest. And the most beautiful. See Mike, I told you: I only hire the best people."

Pens whispered in Trimp's ear.

"We need to sign off here, Mikki. Stay in touch, gorgeous." Trimp said as the SecureNet screen went black.

For her part, Ivanka didn't seem too happy that daddy had just called Mikki Haley gorgeous…

"Simplicity is the ultimate sophistication"
—Leonardo da Vinci

CHAPTER 13

To Get Ahead, We Must Go Backwards

SimpleTown, British Columbia

Less Izmore's former commune, SimpleTown, was growing and expanding at a remarkable pace. The community had actually established several practical colleges for sustainability. People were coming from all over the world and paid $10 per day (if they could) to live, work and train at SimpleTown. There were speciality hands-on courses for: animal husbandry, organic gardening, renewable energy systems, sustainable building techniques, composting and soil maintenance, textile and paper making, food preservation techniques, and forestry and horticulture. Many people spent one week in each discipline in order to practise sustainable living in their own communities.

As SimpleTown was essentially self-sufficient, much of the money paid by students from outside the community went to fund other sustainability or environmental projects in other less-fortunate parts of the world. For example, some of the funds were used to provide transportation and training to bring in students and community leaders from Haiti, Afghanistan, India, Tibet, Bolivia and various African nations. In other cases, experienced Simpletons were sent to these mission fields as "missionaries of sustainability." In almost every case, there was normally a two-way exchange of knowledge. The students who came to SimpleTown often provided ideas to improve systems being used or taught or demonstrated different techniques that could be adapted to suit differing climates, animal species or soil conditions.

Simpleton missionaries had established similar sustainable communities in more than 35 Canadian locations and were expanding into 17 other nations. Canadian Pioneers recently granted land under the Pioneer Project often used information from SimpleTown's website or books to figure out how to get rid of potato bugs, build a water wheel, safely fell a tree, make pickled beets or build a straw-bale house.

Ottawa

The Simpleton Movement was much bigger than the original community itself. For example, the movement had economic implications. It inspired the Finance Minister Less Izmore (a Simpleton founder) to propose and pass a "Simpleton Tax." Essentially, if a good or service were mass produced by machinery, or made of non-organic material, it was subject to the five per cent Simpleton Tax. A plastic and metal chair made in a factory was a good example of an item that was taxed in this manner. The tax raised was then used to subsidize companies or people who made wooden chairs using hand power, hand tools or power derived from renewable sources.

The Simpleton Tax was also applied to food. A frozen bag of imported corn from machinery-operated agribusinesses and food factories was more expensive than locally grown corn from farmers who worked the land with horses and manpower and used no pesticides or chemical fertilizers.

The Simpleton Tax and the Food Additive Tax (FAT), when applied simultaneously to a can of pop, bag of Cheetos, or box of Pizza Pops, essentially priced those unhealthy luxury items beyond reach of the average Canadian consumer.

The FAT was one of the most controversial pieces of legislation the IPP government passed in its early days. In a heated debate in Parliament, Elijah had the following statements in defence of the tax.

"Look, let's be honest with each other. Most people understand that consuming too many processed foods–like pop and Twinkies and chips–is bad for us. The Food Additive Tax is no different than the significant taxes we put on other unhealthy consumer items like cigarettes and alcoholic beverages. Our government has often stepped in and made laws to protect Canadians from making poor decisions. Seat belts and motorcycle helmets? These things used to be optional. But they are now the law because they save lives."

Elijah made quotation marks with his fingers as he continued. "'Freedom' doesn't guarantee individuals the right to make stupid choices, and then expect society to fix things when stupid choices lead to poor results. Because after a lifetime of poor nutritional choices, individuals will become ill, and then they will look to our publicly funded health care system to save them."

Elijah pressed on. "The purpose of this tax is not to make chips and pop and unhealthy processed foods illegal. If you want to eat an unhealthy diet, go ahead. But, if you make that choice, the tax revenue we collect on your purchase will help, in some part, to defray the growing cost of health care. The FAT is a very good way to discourage people from making poor choices all the time." Elijah grinned at the cameras in the House of Commons. "Consider the money you spend on the FAT as a down payment on your future health care needs.

"But there is more to it than that. As explained by our minister of health and by the minister of national revenue, the tax revenue raised by the FAT will be used to subsidize locally produced healthy foods. So that box of Pizza Pops that was five dollars is soon going cost you ten dollars if we can pass this bill." (*Jeers and catcalls from across the floor.*) Elijah waited, smiling, for the jeering to stop.

"But instead of Pizza Pops, you'll soon be able to be able to buy some real food—raised by local farmers and sold in local markets—fresh vegetables, fresh meats, fresh dairy, fresh fruits–for reasonable prices. This is the purpose of the tax. It's an investment in the future health of Canadians. It will, over time, reduce obesity-related illnesses among Canadians."

Elijah appealed now to the viewers at home through the CPAC cameras. "Look, if you work in a factory that makes sugar-coated whammy pops, and similar items that we intend to tax heavily, you are likely worried that this new tax will result in you being laid off. That is a valid concern. So, we are going to work in conjunction with Employment Canada on this issue. And if you lose your job as a result of the FAT, you will have first opportunity at the new jobs created in the local agricultural, food processing and food distribution sectors."

The new PM spoke as if he were in your kitchen or at a coffee shop. "Bottom line, Canada: The foods that make it on this list for the tax are bad for your health if eaten regularly. They are cheap and affordable because they contain lots of sugars, flours, chemicals and toxins. Within a few months, you will be able to afford to buy real whole food again—and that's a win for all of us." Elijah took his seat to cheers and applause from the Independents. Not many of the members of Parliament across the floor jeered this time.

Some unexpected benefits of the Simpleton Movement were remarkable improvements in physical health. People were eating more fresh, healthy local food than previously, primarily because unhealthy foods were heavily taxed and healthy local foods were being subsidized and were, therefore, more affordable. Rather than opening a box of prepackaged instant food, families were spending more time in the kitchen preparing real food, around the kitchen table eating meals together, or even in backyard gardens growing some of their own fruits and vegetables. Family doctors were seeing a reduction in Type 1 and Type 2 diabetes, the average Canadian was a few kilograms lighter, and many had lower blood pressure as a result of their new healthier diet.

The Simpleton lifestyle also improved general mental health for many people. The Internet Tax levied by the Independent People's Party had made it more expensive to spend long hours glued to a cellphone, i-Thing or computer purely for entertainment. (The Internet Tax did not apply to internet usage deemed necessary for work.) Like the FAT, long hours spent on the Internet on social media platforms were deemed an unnecessary luxury, bad for our mental and physical health if overused, and therefore taxed accordingly. People whose faces had been buried in computers and cellphones for years were instead speaking face to face with other humans. As time spent on the internet declined, social media bullying and learning challenges magnified by hours of online brain draining were reduced and interaction with others of our species was on the way up. Internet users who could prove reduced time spent online were given monetary incentives to be reimbursed at social clubs, dance groups, sports teams, music lessons and fitness club memberships—anything, essentially, that would ensure interaction with other people in the actual physical sense. Loneliness, despair and self-imposed internet isolation were gradually being replaced with friendships and social interaction.

Another distant relation of the Simpleton program was the HomeShare program. Before 2019, the Canadian government had taxed any income received from people renting out rooms in their homes. The HomeShare program and tax incentive allowed seniors and empty nesters or anyone with available space to rent out rooms in their principal dwelling without having to worry about a heavy increase on their personal income tax bill. The

HomeShare program also served to lower housing costs for the lowest segment of Canada's wage earners: students, recent graduates, young families, new Canadians and the elderly. Even better, many seniors were exchanging rooms in their house for cooking, cleaning, laundry, maintenance and personal care services. Conversely, some young homeowners were renting out rooms to seniors who provided child minding and domestic services in exchange for that room. Overall, the HomeShare plan made more effective use of existing homes, increased social interaction, reduced loneliness and homelessness, and made affordable housing a reality.

Parrsboro, Nova Scotia

The Magic Bus was visiting a tidal power project on the Bay of Fundy, when Elijah, Dustin Trudel and Harjit Singh rejoined the group.

"Hubba, Hubba!" hollered Benjamin as Juliette leapt into Elijah's arms with a squeal of delight. Dustin and Harjit were greeted warmly (just not quite as warmly as Juliette's greeting to Elijah) by the other ministers.

"I can start again, if you like," the chief engineer offered after the group calmed down. "We were only two minutes into the project overview."

"Sure, if that's OK with the rest of the group?" Elijah responded. Heads were nodding in approval.

"All right, welcome, Mr. Prime Minister, Mr. Trudel and Mr. Singh. So, as we were saying, the tides that flow in and out of the Minas Basin are equal to the flow of all the rivers in the world over 24 hours. We conservatively estimate the tides potential electric output at 2,500 megawatts per day. In layman's terms, that is enough clean renewable power to provide for 100 million people."

Elijah listened to the tidal power pitch with one ear and simultaneously read his briefing notes from Moneypenny:

BRIEFING NOTE:

1. RESISTANCE RALLIES ARE STILL ONGOING. PRESIDENT TRIMP IS SCHEDULING A PRESIDENTIAL ADDRESS TONIGHT FOR 2100 HOURS.
2. 1.45 MILLION US CITIZENS HAVE APPLIED FOR CANADIAN WORK VISAS AND TEMPORARY CITIZENSHIP STATUS IN THE PAST 12 DAYS. IMMIGRATION CANADA HAS INCREASED HIRING SIGNIFICANTLY IN ORDER TO PROCESS DEMANDS EXPEDIENTLY.
3. SENATE APPROPRIATIONS COMMITTEE HAS CONCLUDED ITS STUDY OF MILITARY AIRCRAFT. THE COMMITTEE PROVIDED RECOMMENDATIONS TO PROCEED WITH BUILDING 14,500 BUSH PLANES. THE COMMITTEE RECOMMENDS THE CONTRACT BE AWARDED TO VIKING AIR IN VICTORIA. VIKING AIR HAS PROMISED TO ESTABLISH AIRCRAFT PLANTS IN PORTAGE LA PRAIRIE, MAN., AND DEBERT, NS. THE COMMITTEE'S FILE IS ATTACHED TO THIS BRIEF AS ANNEX B.

4. DART UPDATE. THE INDIAN GOVERNMENT ACCEPTED OUR OFFER OF AID FROM DART. FOUR TEAMS OF 250 PERSONNEL EACH HAVE DEPLOYED TO CENTRAL INDIA. THEY HAVE ESTABLISHED FOUR SEPARATE TEMPORARY RELIEF CAMPS. EACH CAMP IS PROVIDING FOOD, SHELTER, CLEAN WATER AND MEDICAL SERVICES TO 10,000 PERSONS DISPLACED BY FLOODING.
5. YOUR FIANCÉE HAD HER FIRST ULTRASOUND YESTERDAY. CONGRATULATIONS, YOU ARE EXPECTING TWINS!

Elijah looked up from the briefing note with tear-filled eyes. Juliette was smiling through tears as well. She squeezed his hand as the tidal power demonstration continued.

"In individuals, insanity is rare; but in groups, parties, nations and epochs, it is the rule."
– Friedrich Nietzsche

CHAPTER 14

"MAGA, Then KAG"

President Trimp had assembled his Cabinet members (aka his family and friends) in the briefing room. "All right," he said enthusiastically. "Let's MAGA, then KAG!" He clapped for himself, and the group joined in enthusiastically. "I've been thinking over the past few days—and Mike likes my plan. In fact, he said...well, you tell them, Mike."

"It's the best plan ever to Make America Great Again and Keep America Great, Mr. President," Vice President Pens intoned woodenly.

"Thanks, Mike," said Trimp, enthusiastically leading his own applause again. "He's just terrific, isn't he? So, here's my plan. And like I said, it's just the greatest. See, I need to win the upcoming election in November." Trimp paused to allow his minions time to applaud. "That's only eight months away, so we need to get cracking!" Eric and the Trimp siblings and sycophants cheered wildly.

"First, we have to accept an ugly truth." Eric's eyes grew wider with fear. "My good friends at Fox News tell me that

I am taking a beating in the polls." The younger Trimps gasped as if they were one collective being.

"Daddy, that can't be right!" Ivanka shouted petulantly. "You've been Making America Great Again! Why can't these stupid people understand that and just love you and let you Keep America Great?"

"You answered your own question, sweetie," Trimp patiently explained to his daughter. "It's because they are so stupid that they can't appreciate how great I am making America, much greater than 'Crooked Mallory' would have..."

Trimp paused, smiling as his audience chanted "Lock Her Up!" a few times.

"OK, calm down now. So, as you all know, the professional journalists at Fox, especially Shawn Hanratty, are the only media I trust..."

"With good reason, Dad. They are the only journalists who say nice things about you," Eric stated proudly.

"That's right, son. So, when Fox speaks, Donald J. Trimp listens. And Shawn Hanratty told me last night Americans really want three simple things..."

Eric began to applaud wildly.

"Hold on, Eric," Trimp said, shaking his head. "Let me say the three things, and then you can cheer. Better yet, just cheer when Ivanka cheers, OK? We'll call her the head cheerleader..."

Ivanka led them in a rousing, "Gimme a D...D!

"Gimme an A...A!"

When they had finished spelling out D-A-D-Y (the executive assistants in the room knew better than to correct Ivanka's spelling), Trimp began to speak again.

"All right, listen. Daddy tees off in about an hour, so no more cheering till I clap, understood?"

The younger Trimps sat on their hands obediently.

"Now, like I was saying, Shawn told me Americans apparently want three things. They want the internet back, they want to be able to vote for Independent politicians, and they want freedom. Also, Shawn told me that other countries are being stupid, and criticizing America and Daddy." Trimp held up his hands to hush his offspring.

"So, I'm gonna give them those things, and everybody will be happy…Not yet, Ivanka, sweetie," he added hastily, as Ivanka was coiling like a spring to leap out of her chair and lead another cheer.

"So, thing one: We'll have our friends in the 'Space Force'—which I'm very proud I invented by the way, it's just the greatest space force—turn the internet thingys back on. And, we'll still blame the outage on North Korea," he added as an afterthought.

"To Infinity and Beyond!" the chief of the space staff said proudly, standing rigidly to attention and smartly saluting *El Presidente*. Ivanka couldn't hold back any longer, standing and leading the applause wildly. When the applause died down, Trimp continued.

"Then, thing two: We are gonna release all those 'Resistance' people that we just arrested…Not now, Eric. Let Dad explain," Trimp stated, glancing anxiously at his watch. "And finally, thing three: we are gonna let the American people vote for Independent politicians."

The Trimp kids didn't seem excited at the prospect of things two and three. They had all raised their hands to ask questions.

"Now, kids, Mike is gonna explain why all of this makes sense, cuz Daddy needs to get to the golf course and meet a special old friend. I'll make a special announcement tonight about all these things at a 'special' State of the Union Address. And it'll be great. Trust me." Trimp paused briefly to ensure he hadn't forgotten anything and counted off two fingers and one thumb. *Thing one, check. Thing two, check. Thing three, check...*

"OK? Cheer Daddy out, Ivanka."

Ivanka did her best to seem enthusiastic during her "Goooooo, Daddy!" cheer, but she was still thinking about how things two and three could go badly for her and her daddy. *Plus, Mike is a little creepy...*

TRIMP FREES RESISTANCE MEMBERS!, trumpeted the *Daily Bugles* of the world.

SPACE FORCE FIXES INTERNET!, blared other headlines and news personalities.

"Donald Trimp makes America great again and again," Shawn Hanratty was gushing, with support from Fox friends.

With the internet restored, business was booming, as was interaction on social media. There was even a blurry photo of Trimp golfing with what appeared to be a shirtless Vladimir Poutine and several naked Russian women...

"Ladies and Gentlemen, the President of the United States of America," the Sergeant-at-Arms announced in a stentorian voice to the crowd assembled in the House of Representatives.

Donald J. Trimp gave his finest performance in that night's State of the Union Address. He seemed honest, sincere and apologetic. He spoke about healing America. He promised not to nuke Canada (unless provoked again). He extended an olive branch to former enemies like Elijah, Mallory Clifton and the Oobimas. He promised bipartisanship, and open ballots in the upcoming election...

"I want to be optimistic," Michelle Oobima was saying, still sporting some bruises from her recent arrest. "I want to be hopeful. If President Trimp delivers on his promises, and we see Independent politicians' names on ballots, then our nation will have taken one small step forward."

Michelle reluctantly added, "However, Trimp has many sins to atone for. Let's not forget," she reminded, "Donald Trimp tried to annihilate Canada two weeks ago with our entire nuclear arsenal. Let's not forget that Donald Trimp colluded with Russians in 2016, 2018 and is still colluding with Russians now to fix the upcoming election. Let's not forget that Donald Trimp is framing his former staff members for the crimes that Donald Trimp himself is guilty of. Let's not forget Spanky Daniels, or the dozens of women Trimp has abused, harassed and molested over the years. Let's not forget he lined his pockets with NRA blood money while thousands of people were slaughtered on his watch. Let's not forget how he attacked our sacred institutions: the FBI, CIA, our free press and the judiciary. "Let's not forget..."

Hundreds of millions of other people around the world were even less confident and less optimistic of Trimp's honesty.

"President Trimp just freed 2.6 million Americans, rescinded martial law and gave 'The Resistance' what they wanted," Shawn Hannratty said that night. "And all the dumbocrats, libtards and communazis still sat on their hands during his speech. What more can one man do to prove his greatness?"

TRIMP'S FINEST PERFORMANCE? asked the *Tokyo Times*.

CAN AMERICA TRUST TRIMP? The Guardian wondered.

"IN GOD & TRIMP WE TRUST" the Trimpanzees responded, with their newest slogan on bumper stickers, ball caps and T-shirts, available for sale on Trimp's MAGA website.

The next day saw a flurry of activity back at the White House. Trimp orchestrated the activity with rarely seen finesse and skill (from him, at least).

"Mr. President, your executive order to allow Independents free and open access to the ballots!" Vice President Pens announced proudly for the media as he placed the folder in front of the POTUS. Donald Trimp signed the order with his customary flourish as cameras whirred, recording the moment for posterity.

A few moments later, President Trimp met with the three Republicans and three Democrats who composed the most evil secret society in America. The Federal Election Commission's sole purpose was to ensure that Americans could only choose between Republican or Democrat candidates. Any third-party choice was extremely hazardous to the health of a duopoly. The recently signed executive order directing the FEC to allow Independent candidates access to ballots was on 45's desk.

"Mr. President, the diligent and unsung work of the FEC has kept our two parties in power since 1780," the senior Republican on the committee stated bluntly. "We see this executive order as very dangerous to American freedom and democracy."

President Trimp smiled sadly. "Me too. I don't like losing. But I had to give, uhhh, Mike, you tell them. It's a terrific deal. Just great."

Vice President Pens continued on Trimp's behalf.

"Gentlemen, President Trimp had to give the American people the illusion that they could have another choice in November. He had to make a deal with the devil to stop the protests and get people back to work." As the VP continued to address the FEC, President Trimp slipped away to watch some Fox News in the corner. Mike Pens just kept speaking as if that were normal behaviour.

"Your people at the state level can still make the application process somewhat difficult for Independents. Just make sure to give the gradual impression of progress—let people see Independent politicians' names slowly appearing on ballots. Our Republican and Democratic candidates are still far better funded and organized than the Independents. President Trimp and I are very confident that the next president of the United States will be a Republican or

Democrat. In either case, we all win. These Independents have no platform, no history. We have some mutual friends with deep pockets in both our parties who will begin attack ads on individual Independents shortly…"

"Like this one—look, look,!" the 45th POTUS was shouting at the television excitedly. The commercial showed an actor who looked exactly like Michelle Oobima lighting a pile of guns on fire.

"Michelle Oobima wants to take away your guns, America!" a patriotic voice was booming. The next screen showed Donald Trimp with Todd Nugent at a firing range, cutting a tree in half with two assault rifles. Both men were wearing camo, MAGA hats and clearly having a wonderful time. The camera zoomed in on Trimp.

"I won't take away your guns, America. I'm Donald J. Trimp, and I approved this message. Vote Trimp in 2020 to Keep America Great!"

For the first weeks of early March, Trimp remained in Mar-a-Lago, laying low and tweeting nonsense. America was rudderless and hesitant, which was it how had been since the Trimp Inauguration. The majority of Americans (except for the 22 per cent of the population who were committed Trimpanzees and MAGAts) had been convinced long ago that Trimp was criminally insane.

The media buzzed like bees with talk of impending impeachments, but everybody seemed paralyzed. Most people were just sick of the political bullshit and seemed eager for the upcoming election.

The Republican Party was in rough shape, with the primaries looming in the near future. So far, the known candidates included: Donald J. Trimp, "L'il Marco" Rubion, Mikki Haley, "Sloppy" Steve Bannin, Sarah Palon, "Borin' Jeb" Busch, Todd Cruz and Todd Nugent.

The Democratic National Convention looked a bit more hopeful. "Uncle" Joe Baden and young Jim Kennedy were the front runners, followed by Andre Cuomo and some lesser-known representatives and senators. Kamala Morris, Kristin Gillislee and Elizabeth Worrin were three very high-profile politicians whom the Democrats had hoped would run in the 2020 primary. Instead, they had left the Democratic party to join the Independent People's Party.

The Independent politicians were miles ahead of either traditional party. They had already selected Michelle Oobima as their leader and Dwain John-Stone as her vice-presidential running mate.

The Independent candidates were a powerful team. They were a mix of experienced, respected politicians from both traditional parties already in Senate and House seats. There were successful businesspersons, a few celebrities, retired athletes, farmers, doctors, welders, teachers and fishermen.

"I've been criticizing and satirizing politicians for many years now," comedienne Sarah Silverstein said in a press conference called "Meet the Independents." "So I'm gonna do my very best to represent my constituents with honesty and integrity...Yes, *New York Times*?"

"Ms. Silverstein, that's a bit cliché. Don't you think that it is every politician's intent to represent their constituents with honesty and integrity?"

"Maybe at first. But that's hard to do if you take large political donations from the NRA–like my Republican opponent–and from RamJack Corp–like my Democratic opponent."

The Independent candidates were following the lead of the Canadian Independent People's Party. They were not accepting contributions from corporations. They were communicating their platform via social media. They tracked their costs and expenses to the penny and posted them online.

In Gallup's March poll regarding the upcoming election:

- 11 per cent of Americans expressed blind unwavering faith in Donald Trimp and the Republican party and Republican Jesus;
- 23 per cent intended to vote for a Democratic candidate;
- 55 per cent intended to vote Independent; and,
- 11 percent were undecided.

After President Trimp's promise to allow citizens to vote for Independents, most Americans gave up the Resistance Rallies and tried to resume living a normal life. "I can't lose any more time from work. I've got a family to feed, and the kids need to get back to school," was a common refrain among regular people.

The Federal Election Commission, meanwhile, was doing its best to stall putting those third names on ballots, while also pretending to be upfront and honest. "There is a process, and that process can't be rushed. It takes time to ensure rigorous background checks and proper vetting," Independent candidates were told.

Trimp was a master at this game. He wrote the book on appearing genuine to customers, while simultaneously stiffing, conning and lying to: builders, contractors, suppliers, realtors, tenants, and all unsatisfied customers.

Remember? Chapter Four of *The Art of The Steal. The Nine Steps to Success!*:

1. Hire (but don't pay) really good criminal lawyers and criminal accountants. You'll need them later.
2. Develop/design a great product. (Hint: It doesn't really have to be great. You just need to call it great. Make it overseas—brown and yellow people are hard, efficient, low-cost workers.)
3. Sell the product. Get the client's money. Take pictures of yourself with gorgeous women and rich, famous people enjoying your product. (You might have to promise to pay the women for this part.) (But don't pay them—just promise to introduce them to producers.)
4. Stall paying your bills.
5. Sell more product. Get more client's money. Take more pictures (repeat step 3).
6. Don't pay your bills. (Listen, only schmucks pay their bills. Use your lawyers and accountants to stall in court/sue landlords or suppliers for poor product or service to reduce cost.)
7. Sell more product. (Repeat steps 3 and 5.)

8. When you can stall no longer, fold up shop, declare bankruptcy. (This is where your criminal lawyers and accountants earn their money. Pay them a little, or you'll never find any more lawyers.) Sha-Zam! You have made all the profit and paid little or nothing to your suppliers and employees.
9. Start new business. Repeat.

From 2017 to 2020, when Trimp was president of the USA, his customers and suppliers were the American people. And the good people of America were sick and tired of being lied to and conned by Donald Trimp.

"We are taking a ton of heat from people at the state and district level," the FEC chairman was telling Mr. Trimp. "We can't stall people too much longer. People are starting to mutter about these 'Resistance Rallies' again."

Donald Trimp appeared to be hearing his FEC visitors. He looked genuinely concerned, nodding his head at all the appropriate times. *Melanie isn't getting any younger,* he was thinking, as he looked at a family photo of them on his desk. *Dammit. Why is it I can't marry Ivanka?*

Trimp had heard enough. He prided himself on being a man of action, and he now realized that action was urgently required.

"Now, Gentlemen, you've been doing a great job. But it's my job to worry about the American people," he said to his visitors, rising abruptly. He nodded at his security team, which opened the door.

"And nobody cares more or worries more for the American people better than me. I'm really a terrific worrier," he continued passionately. "Maybe the best worrier ever. The doctor here said I worry way more than Oobima ever did. But like I said, it's my job to worry. Now you fellows need to keep stalling those Independent applications just a little longer. Because if the Independents get their names on those ballots, it's the end of American freedom as we know it. And nobody loves freedom more than me, by the way. Oobima and 'Crooked Mallory' hated freedom. Trust me, in a couple days, America will forget all about the Independent party."

The FEC members looked skeptical as Trimp backslapped them out the door.

When his guests had departed, Donald J. Trimp picked up his *"Super Top-Secret"* phone.

It was actually the same unsecured cellphone he used for all his tweets and calls. He just liked to imagine it was *Super Top Secret.*

"Take as many vacations as you can. You can always make money. You can't always make memories."
—Unknown

CHAPTER 15

Spring Break

Ottawa, Ontario

"In a moment, we'll recess," Elijah told the members of the raucous Canadian Parliament. "We've been working hard here since New Years. And we've accomplished a lot of really great things. So, for the next few days, chill. Rest. Relax. Recharge those batteries. We'll see everyone back here in 11 days." The members of the House of Parliament cheered like high school kids at Spring Break. It was, in fact, Spring Break for students in some states and provinces.

During the Independent People's Party tenure as the Government of Canada, the number of days worked and individual workloads for politicians had increased, pay had been reduced by 25 per cent and pensions reduced by 50 per cent.

"Notwithstanding the pay cuts and increased workload, I just described, morale among parliamentarians and staff has never been higher," reported Peter Bridgeman of the CBC. "And I've been reporting on Parliament since 1972."

Montreal, Quebec

Dustin and Sophia Trudel, along with their three children, Xanadu, Estelle and Eugenie, were getting ready for a working holiday in Vietnam. As the minister of foreign affairs, Dustin would be the one "officially" working. Sophia liked to remind Dustin that "minding adventurous 12-, 10- and five-year-old kids was likely more difficult than being minister of anything." Dustin had meetings scheduled with his Vietnamese counterparts over a three-day period. His ticket and room were taxpayer funded. All his family's expenses were rigorously and painstakingly kept visibly separate.

(Trudel, while in his early days as prime minister, had been harshly criticized by the opposition in 2017 for a family holiday with the Aga Khan at his private island in the Bahamas. Dustin was reminded of this every time he travelled with his family.)

"Like all of us, I make mistakes. I plan to learn from my mistakes and not repeat them."

While the former prime minister was in meetings, Sophia and the Trudel children were going to visit Vietnam like millions of other tourists did each year. Then the family had a glorious week together at a beachside resort.

The Trudels were a very photogenic family. Eugenie normally made the job much easier for the press. "Eugenie is a natural-born ham," Dustin often said. The press followed them to, then into, the airport, with Eugenie mugging for the camera the whole way.

"Dad, make her stop," Xanadu quietly begged at the airport, as his little sister continued her play-by-play analysis of their pending trip for a news camera. "People are gonna think we're the most dysfunctional family."

Dustin smiled patiently. "Xanadu, I have bad news. Some people are going to think that we are a dysfunctional family no matter what your little sister does."

Hanoi, Vietnam

Twenty-three hours later, Eugenie and the Trudel Family were once again charming the press, this time at a formal reception and garden party hosted at the historic presidential palace in Hanoi. Eugenie made quick friends with the Vietnamese presidents' grandson. The early favourite for Associated Press photo of the year was Eugenie Trudel and Trần Đại Quang in mud-covered formal attire, hugging two Vietnamese pot-bellied pigs.

For the next three days, Dustin and the Canadian envoy discussed trade and immigration with their Vietnamese counterparts while Sophia and the Trudel children visited Hanoi. Eugenie and Trần Đại Quang had become inseparable allies in mischief. The pair plotted their next adventures in a patois of French, Vietnamese and English. The children had become such good friends that Sophia convinced the Quang Family to join them for a week at the beach at Nha Trang.

The beaches at Nha Trang are world renowned. Dustin, Sophia, the Trudels and the Quang Family had a wonderful time. "This was the best vacation ever," Eugenie charmingly told the Vietnamese press from the Hanoi airport. "We wrestled sharks and octopusses and rode oliphants…"

Springfield, Ontario

Charley and Dorothy Shackleton were not beach resort people. "Hah. Yes, I can see Charley now on a beach in coveralls and rubber boots," Dorothy had laughed when friends had asked them about their vacation plans. "Charley is more of a staycation guy. His idea of a relaxing day would be ploughing a field, feeding chickens and shovellin' horse shit."

Charley missed being on the farm when Parliament was in session. "I think you missed Fred more than you missed me," Dorothy teased him as Charley and his furry friend renewed their acquaintance in the kitchen.

Dorothy had been busy on the farm in Charley's absence. She had taken on a Pioneer family from Cleveland to help her work the farm. The Smiths had come to Canada during the Great Canadian Blackout and never bothered to return home. Dorothy was a good teacher. She had gained a lot of pioneering knowledge from her years at SimpleTown.

Under her direction, the Smith Family had doubled the number of chickens. They were selling free-range eggs and chickens at a nearby farmers' market. They had built a fair-sized greenhouse, which was full of seedlings: peppers, tomatoes, eggplants, squashes, melons of all shapes and sizes, all destined to be sold in garden supply centres in southern Ontario later that spring.

Chevonne Smith worked as a cook at a nearby seniors' residence. Her husband Darnell maintained the equipment at a water-powered hemp mill a few miles further down the road. The mill produced hemp fabric, which was then used to make clothes.

They were also beginning to harvest sap from an old sugar bush at the east quarter of Charley's property. "Makin' maple syrup was always my favourite thing to do on the farm," Charley said to the Smith boys. "But I never found the time to do it last year," he continued, as he showed the boys how to harness an old work horse called Delilah to a sled. "OK. Now she's all hooked up. Has either one of you fellers got your driver's licence for Delilah?"

As Charley showed the boys how to guide the old work horse, he explained what would happen. Delilah's job was to pull the sled through the woods. Charley, Dorothy and the Smith boys would collect buckets of sap from each tree and pour the sap into milk cans on the sled.

"Then we pour that sap in a big 50-gallon pan, and build a fire underneath that pan, and boil that sap down into the sweetest most delicious syrup."

Mistawasis First Nation, Saskatchewan

Benjamin Big Canoe and Danni Grey Eyes were having a time in Mistawasis. The band put out the biggest possible welcome mat for their hometown hero. After all, Danni Grey Eyes was their former band chief who had gone to become a federal member of Parliament and minister of Aboriginal affairs. Oh, and she had a smokin' hot boyfriend.

Benjamin (like most boyfriends) was nervous to meet Danni's parents and extended family for the first time. That nervousness quickly faded. He was immediately drafted onto the tribal hockey team and scored five goals in three playoff games against a cross-province rivals. In between hockey games, he and his new friends caught an amazing number of pike and muskie.

"I never dreamed that pike got this big," he said to Danni's father. "Or tasted this good," he added, sampling some more of the previous day's catch that had been smoked over a slow fire.

During their stay, Mistawasis also hosted a powwow, with attendees and entertainers from all over the Great Plains. There was live music, and Aboriginal games, and dancing, and sweat lodges and smoke ceremonies and traditional food.

Pemmican, smoked goose, bison bannock burgers with Saskatoon berry BBQ sauce, caribou stew, elk tacos, wild rice risotto…

"I forgot how good our food was," Benjamin told Danni dreamily through a haze of smoke and steam that night in the sweat lodge.

"Benjamin, that's my *kokum*," Danni told him, laughing from the other side of the lodge. "She doesn't speak English. Tell her in Cree."

Benjamin managed to stammer out something about "good food" in Cree to Danni's grandmother. He spoke English, French and Ojibwa, but had only begun learning Cree that week.

The old woman laughed heartily and replied very quickly in Cree. The people in the sweat lodge broke out in gentle laughter.

"Sorry, uh, what did she say?"

"She said 'thank you,'" Danni replied from somewhere in the mist. The sweat lodge was spinning a little for Benjamin. *Man, it's hot in here...*

"Why did everybody laugh if she just said, 'thank you?'"

"She said the heat must be getting to you if you mistook her for me, cuz she's 87. Then she said she wishes she was young again 'cause she thinks you are very handsome."

The line was just as funny the second time around in English. Benjamin was a little embarrassed, but that feeling passed quickly as he began to float.

It felt good to float.

He smiled and let it happen.

Havana, Cuba

Elijah and his fiancée Juliette Sparks were on a working holiday. In her role as minister of youth, Juliette was the headline speaker at a youth conference at Havana's main university that was attended by students from more than 80 countries. Juliette was an engaging speaker: fiery, passionate, sympathetic, courageous, convincing and often controversial. As a 24-year-old who had recently graduated university with a degree in international development, she felt right at home.

She didn't just deliver a canned speech and leave though. Juliette stayed at the university for the whole three days of the conference. She participated in workshops on everything from green technology to ageism to quiet revolutions.

Elijah was also busy. He attended a conference of Caribbean leaders. It was the first time that a leader of a non-Caribbean nation had been invited. "I'm really honoured to be here among you," he told his fellow prime ministers and presidents. "And I'm thrilled to be somewhere warm, because it's three below zero and raining in Ottawa today."

Elijah had been under the microscope of public scrutiny for many years. As the host of *Power to the People*, most of that scrutiny resulted in positive feedback. The show was the most popular TV show ever aired in Canada. While Elijah's views were radical, people understood, (and Elijah often flippantly told them): "If you don't like what I'm saying, change the channel."

Being a politician was different, however. Canadians couldn't change the channel, and some of the bills and legislation that Elijah and the IPP had passed enraged a lot of people. He wasn't loved by people who had a big stake in the oil and gas industry, for example. That's an understatement. They really hated him.

He met some of those people on the second day of the Caribbean leaders' conference. A Canadian oil company was pitching the benefits of offshore oil drilling to the Trinidadians and Barbadians when Elijah quietly entered the room.

"Umm, why are you here?" the chief executive officer asked bluntly.

"I'm at the conference as a guest of the Caribbean leaders," Elijah replied deadpan. "Please, don't let me interrupt your brief."

"I'll start again when you leave the room."

"Well, I'd like to hear your brief. You represent a Canadian oil and gas company. I'm always interested in matters of international trade and development…"

"Bullshit, you are. Your crazy tree huggin' socialist government has ruined the oil and gas industry in Canada, and now you're here trying to make sure that these people can't profit from a rich natural resource."

"Not at all. I came here to listen to your brief. But you don't seem happy to see me here, so I'll go in a minute," Elijah said to the CEO. He then turned to face the audience. "I would just encourage the folks listening to this brief to consider the safety and environmental concerns that offshore drilling could present in such a fragile ecosystem, and to have a good look at this company's safety record."

SimpleTown, British Columbia

Less Izmore was thrilled to be back in his former commune. SimpleTown had grown tremendously over the past few years. He was pleased to see that all of the original buildings they had built in 1988 were still standing. Many had been added on to and expanded, but he could still see his handiwork and that of the original Simpletons in every rock wall and hand-hewn beam.

"There's five of us original Simpletons from 1988 left here," an old friend called Heckle was telling him.

They were in the meeting hall, looking at the logbooks and registries. Every time new people arrived, they signed into the logbook if they intended to become Simpletons. The page for 1988 had Less, Dorothy, Heckle and Jekyll as the first four members in April. By August that year, there were 23 more members. A year later, there were 85 Simpletons, then 137…

Slightly more than 3,000 people had called SimpleTown home over the years. A small percentage only stayed a few weeks. A greater percentage of people stayed a year or two. A surprisingly large number stayed for much longer. As a former elder and co-founder of SimpleTown, Less knew almost all of them, except for those newcomers who had arrived since he had been elected as a member of parliament.

"More than 400 children have been born here," Less said proudly, flipping through the Registry of Births. "That's an amazing number."

"A lot of the kids who were born here have never left," Heckle's brother Jekyll added happily. "And many of those who do go away are training other people how to live a simple life."

A silhouette walked past the window and waved, but Less couldn't make out who it was. The setting sun was in his eyes. "Speaking of Simpleton missionaries," Jekyll continued, "here's a couple now who just came home last week…"

"Uncle Less!" Susanna shrieked as she bounded into the older man's open arms.

KT hugged Less as Less hugged Susanna. "Hey. we thought you'd be happy to see us," Susanna teased, wiping at Less's tears with a dirty shirtsleeve.

"Susanna, I've never been happier," Less murmured, smiling. "These are tears of joy, child."

After a few minutes, Susanna ran off to help in the bakery, her favourite job "from way back when I was little."

Heckle and Jekyll had drifted outside to give Less and KT some space.

"Are you back for good, KT?"

"I think so,' she replied solemnly. "This might be the only place Susanna has ever felt truly safe." She was quiet for a minute. "And we missed it something awful."

Less nodded knowingly. He tried to speak, but couldn't, and wiped away fresh tears as KT hugged him again.

*There was given to him a mouth speaking arrogant
words and blasphemies, and authority to act
for forty-two months was given to him.*
—Revelation 13.5, New American Standard Bible

CHAPTER 16

"This Is Not A Drill"

Washington, the Pentagon

"Vladimir? Hey, it's Donald here on my *Super Top-Secret phone.*"

Pause.

"Trimp. And, yes, of course, I'm still the president, again."

Pause

"No, those stories are Fake News. Hey, new topic, how about that golf course at Mar-a-Lago? Isn't that just the greatest?"

Pause

"C'mon, you know how the media loves to lie. And I would never cheat at golf. Golf is sacred to me, like a wife, or porn star, or Playmate hooker."

Pause

"Hey, listen, I need a favour. Remember that thing we discussed on the golf course?"

Pause

"No, the other thing, from a country near you. I have a terrific offer for you if you can help me with that."

Pause

"That's just great. I'll make it worth your time and effort, I promise. It's gonna be tremendous for both of us. Just terrific. Trust me…"

CHEYENNE MOUNTAIN. APRIL 9, 2020. 0311 RMT

After years of training on and watching air defence systems scopes, Air Force Sgt Marion Jackson had to blink rapidly and look twice to believe what she was seeing. As per her years of training at USAF technical schools, she hit the red button. The red button sounds a very loud claxon, and sets a red light spinning. There is nothing like a claxon and a spinning red light to get your heart racing if you work at Cheyenne Mountain.

"Whattya got, Jackson?" the officer of the watch demanded instantly.

"Sir, our satellites just picked up three ICBM launches from North Korea."

"Intended targets?"

Sgt. Jackson tracked trajectory and vectors. "Honolulu, LA and Dallas, Sir."

"Time till impact?"

"Fifteen minutes for Hawaii, 28 minutes for LA, 32 minutes for Dallas."

The USAF colonel picked up a red phone. "DEFCON ONE. I repeat. We are at DEFCON ONE. Three Incoming ICBMs. Point of origin, North Korea."

Within 30 seconds, the flash message had been sent.

One minute later, aircraft were scrambling from every USAF base and every aircraft carrier in the US Navy.

At a location 235 nautical miles northwest of Pearl Harbour, Commander Richard Clark of *USS Annapolis*, a ballistic missile submarine, had his ops team locking in coordinates.

"Locked in on one."

"Fire."

"Locked in on two."

"Fire."

"Locked in on three."

"Fire."

On hundreds of ops screens across a variety of NATO countries, in *USS Annapolis*, and Cheyenne Mountain, and the Pentagon, at Pacific Fleet Command, on-watch personnel literally held their breath as the missiles streaked toward each other.

"Splash one, Sir!" Sgt. Jackson reported as the missile from *Annapolis* intercepted a Korean missile. The ops room cheered wildly. The officer of the watch raised his hands for silence and barked, "Pipe down, people. We still have two missiles incoming. Stay focused."

"Splash two, Sir!" The longest 30 seconds ever ticked by...

"Splash three, Sir!"

"Three cheers for the United States Navy!" shouted the colonel. "Hip hip..."

"...Hooray!" responded ops rooms enthusiastically around the world. But not aboard *USS Annapolis*.

The ashen-faced crew in the *Annapolis* ops room was (very) quietly intoning the "Submariners Prayer," together:

> "O Father, hear our prayer to Thee,
> For your humble servants, beneath the sea
> In the depths of oceans, as oft they stray,
> So far from night, so far from day
> We would ask your Guiding Light to glow,
> To make their journey safe below
> Please oft times grant them patient mind,
> Then 'ere the darkness won't them blind
> They seek thy protection from the deep,
> Please grant them peace
> when 'ere they sleep
> Of their homes and loved ones far away,
> We ask you care for them each day
> Until they surface once again,
> To drink the air and feel the rain
> We ask your guiding hand to show,
> A safe progression sure and slow
> Dear Lord, please hear our prayer to thee,
> For your humble servants beneath the sea."

Cdr. Richard Clark looked proudly as his crew and spoke quietly. "Well done, Silent Service. Let's keep our heads up. This may not be over. Officer of the Watch, make our depth 60 feet, steer 130, speed four knots."

AN ACT OF WAR shouted headlines around the world.

@realDonaldTrimp: L'il Rocket Man, prepare for some fire and fury!

Commander Pacific Fleet (COMPACFLT) had already been on high alert. Three aircraft carriers and all their associated naval firepower (enough to melt North Korea into a flat glass puddle) had been operating just off the Korean Peninsula for several months. All they needed was the word from the commander in chief.

I don't hear any lefties or commies whining about fair elections and Resistance Rallies this morning, Donald Trimp smiled at himself in the mirror. *Nothing like a war to distract the peasants,* he thought, as he flipped off Fox News. He had a meeting with his new Joint Chiefs at 0800. *Plenty of time.* His little blue pills were just kicking in as he knocked on Melanie's door. *If one pill is good, three must be…three times as good.*

It's a great day to be Donald J. Trimp, Donald J. Trimp thought to himself. *And Donald J. Trimp's wife.*

Melanie looked puzzled, but pasted on what she hoped was a smile, as she opened her door.

Hmmm, funny. The Donald only calls once or twice a year, thank goodness. Ahh, I guess it's the price I pay for fame and fortune.

Vladivostok, Russia

Just as Donald J. Trimp was (literally) knocking on Melanie's door, Interpol and the Russian Federal Security Service arrested Vladmir Poutine. A Russian crab fishing boat out of Vladivostok had videotaped a Russian submarine launching the three missiles from North Korean waters. The video evidence was irrefutable. It showed a submarine with Russian insignia surface, launch three missiles in rapid succession, and quickly descend beneath the waves.

President Poutine was arrested for ordering a Russian submarine to launch three nuclear missiles at the USA. The Russian security service had been listening to his phones for several months. They suggested that many more charges were pending. The international community was justifiably concerned and confused. Why had the Russians tried to make it appear as if North Korea launched the missiles?

It's pretty big news whenever one country attacks another country with nuclear weapons. It's even bigger, crazier news when the attacking country tries to make it look like someone else did it.

The White House

"This is Shawn Hanratty with breaking Fox News!" Hanratty shouted from Melanie's TV. The FLOTUS knew that the POTUS needed to hear good news about himself 24 /7.

Fox generally provided her husband with that good news. It was just standard operating procedure that Fox was on every TV in the White House and Mar-a-Lago (the Southern White House) all the time.

"President Trimp, it wasn't North Korea that attacked us," Hanratty continued breathlessly. "It was the Russians!" For the past two years, Hanratty had just been addressing Trimp directly, rather than speaking to a TV audience.

Oh, thank God for Fox, sighed Melanie, as The Donald moved away from her, and stood transfixed in front of the screen clad only in tighty whities.

Hanratty continued. "The Russians report they have just arrested Vladimir Poutine! Our guest is recently retired

US Admiral William McHale, former Chief of Naval Staff. Adm. McHale, why would the Russians attack us? And why try to make it appear as if the attack came from North Korea?"

Adm. McHale began to answer Hanratty, but Trimp's eyes were glazing over. He reached for his trusty Twitter phone.

The news of Vladimir Poutine's arrest made Donald J. Trimp even more scatterbrained and unfocused than normal. The past three years of being criticized by people he could not control came gushing out of 45 like liquid nonsense from a high-pressure hate hose.

From the First Lady's bedroom he went on a 7 a.m. Twitterstorm the likes of which will never be equalled. Here's a sample.

Brace yourself.

@realDonaldTrimp: I never trusted L'il Vladimir Poutine. Don't believe anything he says. He will start lying bigly very soon. There was no cofeve! #Russia&KoreaNukeEmBoth #TrimpMAGA2020 #ThereIsNoPeePeeTape

@realDonaldTrimp: A woman I have never met is on Fake CNN news saying I grabbed her hoohoo at a funeral in Florida in 2018. Never happened. I mean, look at her! But Lyin' Barrack Oobima? His name in Kenyan means pussy grabber. #1stKenyanPresident #ShowUsTheBirthCertificate

@realDonaldTrimp: Crooked Mallory 'Crooked Mallory' Clifton sold mucho uranium to L'il Vladimir Poutine over the years. And you know what people do with uranium, right? Things like bombs and other…bad things. #CrookedMallory #LockHerUp #TrimpThatBitch #INeverLose

@realDonaldTrimp: Shawn Hanratty of Fox News knows the truth. He reports the Russians and L'il Vladimir Poutine have been colluding with Soviet Canuckistan for years to overthrow the USA. #NukeEmTillTheyGlow #NukeEmAll&LetGodSortEmOut #WhyHaveNukesIfNotToNukeStuff

@realDonaldTrimp: VP Pence and myself will address the crowd tomorrow at the National Prayer Breakfast. God will continue to bless America (but not sinners like Michelle Oobima or Jews like Barney Saunders). Americans are God's Chosen People! #TrimpMAGA2020 #InGodAndTrimpWeTrust #RepublicanJesus&NRA

@realDonaldTrimp: @SpankyDaniels @17AssaultedWomen Really? I never even met, let alone touched, Spanky Daniels or the 17 women in this group lawsuit. @WaPo @NYTimes @SarahSilverStein @ChelseaChandler: Lawyer up, Bitches. Here comes @RoyKohn! #SicEmRoy #AllFakeNews #IAmAboveTheLaw

@realDonaldTrimp: my meeting with @QueenElizabeth will be postponed, again, cuz Ole Crybaby Liz is worried I'll be too popular and replace her on the throne! The British people love me! #OffWithHerHead #FakeQueen #YourFootballSucks #IAmTheTrueKing

@realDonaldTrimp: thanks @FOX News. "A study by hand experts at the Smithsonian Institution concluded today that Donald Trimp has the largest hands of any US president or any world leader ever. #BigHands=BigYouKnow #SuckItOobima #SuckItDubya #SuckItBillClifton

@realDonaldTrimp: those whiny students need to STFU about gun reform and get back to school! Guns are America's God-Given Right iaw the 2cnd Amendment. ##FromMyColdDeadHands #IBlameTheDems #LousyParents #NRAPatriots! #ArmTheStudents

@realDonaldTrimp: Americans know better than to be tricked into voting Independent! @MichelleOobima will take away your guns and make you pay for welfare & HealthCare! @MichelleOobima is weak on crime and will give women rights over their vaginas! #VoteTrimp2020 #PatrioticWomenShouldn'tVote #NRAPatriots

There were many more tweets from @realDonaldTrimp, but Twitter had to delete them for content that included extreme hate speech, racism and sexism. Although it was difficult for Trimp to shock people in 2020, this glimpse into his mind really scared most normal people.

Other charges against Poutine and his associates later that morning included: assassination of political opponents at home and abroad, murder and attempted murder, international money laundering, tampering with foreign and domestic elections, obstruction of domestic and international justice, spying, wiretapping, torture, war crimes, human trafficking, profiting from prostitution, profiting from child slavery, blackmail…There were more charges, but these were the major ones.

In accordance with the Russian Constitution, Prime Minister Dimitri Modvodov took over as interim president, and promised an election by mid October.

Poutine flipped on Trimp at the first mention of old school interrogation. (His former KGB subordinates were rumoured to be disappointed that they didn't get to practise on their former boss and instructor.) Vladimir Poutine had a lot of dirt on Donald Trimp. He testified on videotape, and under oath. He admitted to colluding with Trimp to fix the Republican primary and the 2016 and 2018 elections. He admitted to laundering billions of rubles and euros and dollars through Trimp Inc.'s various holdings. He implicated Trimp's entire crime family as complicit and provided specific details.

Two hours after Vladimir Poutine's arrest, Donald J. Trimp was arrested by Robert Miller Jr in the First Lady's bedroom. (It actually took White House staff 30 minutes to locate the president. No one had ever seen him in Melanie's bedroom, so it was the last place they looked.)

"You realize these charges won't stick," Trimp spat angrily at Miller. "I'm the goddammed president of the United States. I own the judges, I own the Department of Justice, I…"

"You have the right to remain silent," replied Miller sternly, cutting him off with his Miranda rights. Textbook Robert Miller Jr.

Remember, Robert Miller Jr was a man who exuded trust, honour, integrity, truth, courage, dignity and loyalty to the Constitution of the United States. In every way imaginable, he demonstrated the exact opposite character traits of Donald Trimp.

Robert Miller Jr was a graduate of Princeton who served as a Marine Corps officer during the Vietnam War. During that conflict, he was awarded the Bronze Star Medal for heroism and a Purple Heart.

After serving his country with honor in Vietnam, Miller studied law at the University of Virginia. Following his studies, he was appointed as an Assistant US Attorney in San Francisco, as a United States Attorney, as United States Assistant Attorney General, and as US Deputy Attorney General.

In 2001, President George Busch appointed Miller (a conservative Republican) as head of the Federal Bureau of Investigation. In 2011, President Barrack Oobima extended that term by two years, making Miller the longest-serving director of the FBI since J. Edgar Whoover.

In May 2017, Deputy Attorney General Rod Rosenbloom appointed Miller to head the Special Counsel investigation of Russian interference in the 2016 US election, including any links between Vladimir Poutine's government and Donald Trimp's campaign.

You see, Robert Miller Jr was the only person that Trimp actually feared. A scan of Trimp's Twitter account history shows that Trimp nicknamed and attempted to smear and humiliate all his enemies (except Miller) on Twitter: Crooked Mallory, Crazy Barrack, Slobberin' Joe, Sloppy Steve, Cryin' Adam, Pocohontas, etc.

Trimp never dared attack Miller openly because Trimp knew he had committed crimes, and Trimp knew that Miller knew about those crimes. It was only a matter of time (#MillerTime), before the doggedly determined litigator brought the Trimp crime family to justice. One of the most popular hashtag phrases on Twitter throughout

Trimp's reign of terror and Miller's Special Counsel investigation had been:

@RealDonaldTrimp: #TickTock #WhatTimeIsIt? #MillerTime

As Miller was arresting Trimp, 43 members of the Trimp Administration were also arrested.

A partial list included: Don Jr, Eric, Ivanka, her husband Jared, Mike Pens, Sarah Huckleberry Slanders, the attorney general, the party leader, the party whip, multiple departmental secretaries, various complicit senior GOP personnel and three supreme court justices.

The Bible Belt Chapel, North Carolina

Some hard-core Trimpanzees, however, remained fiercely loyal to Trimp's cause right up to and beyond his sorry end.

A few evangelicals like Frankland Graham continued to defend Trimp as "God's Chaos Candidate."

"Throughout history, God has used powerful men like Mr. Trimp to do His work here on earth," Graham thundered from his pulpit.

"God is not a communist Jew like Barney Saunders.

"God is not an immoral Muslim woman like Michelle Oobima.

"God is not a papist Catholic like the Kennedys.

"God is not a prophet of Islam like Mohammed or Allah, preaching hate and intolerance.

"God is love.

"God is working through Donald J. Trimp, a patriotic American, to do his good work here on earth.

"God, through Donald Trimp, will cast out the sinners among us!

"God, through Donald Trimp, will smite the non-believers!

"God, through Donald Trimp, will vanquish our enemies, and the righteous among us will be victorious!

"Let us bow our heads in prayer."

Washington DC

The United States Constitution clearly defines the lines of succession should the president be unable to finish their term.

Normally, the vice president would take over (but Mike Pens had just been arrested).

If the president and vice president are both incapacitated, the House speaker assumes the presidency. So, for the second time in two months, Nancy Pillosi was sworn in as the 46th POTUS.

President Pillosi appointed Cory Booker, a Democratic senator, as her vice president.

In the House of Representatives, Congress selected Jim Kennedy, a young Democratic congressman, as the Speaker of the House.

Meanwhile, as Pillosi's administration quietly took steps to form effective government, the media still clamoured for news of Trimp. *Quiet, Thoughtful, Deliberate Politician* wasn't much of a headline, after all.

Trimp, for his part, had always loved the stage and had desperately needed attention his whole life.

Trimp's polar opposite, Robert Miller Jr, did his best to avoid the glare of those lights. Robert Miller Jr was not an emotional man, nor a theatrical one.

He reluctantly met with the press the day after the Trimp Administration was arrested.

"Mr. Miller, do you feel relieved that this Special Counsel is nearly finished its mandate?"

"No," Robert Miller replied impassively. "Because we're not done yet."

"Do you have a time frame when the Special Counsel might be finished?"

"No."

"Mr. Miller, can you explain how this case was built and why it took so long? For example, who took a plea bargain and cooperated with your counsel? Can you tell us who flipped on who?"

"No, I can't explain that yet, because some of the investigations are still underway," Miller replied dryly. "I can tell you that each case is very complex because we are working with Interpol and various Russian security forces. We still need to proceed slowly, methodically and professionally to ensure that we follow the rule of law. To try and hurry the procedure now would be to risk three years of painstaking effort by our team." Robert Miller Jr looked as resolute as a slab of granite.

"That is a mistake I'm not willing to make."

A well regulated militia, being necessary to the security of a free state, the right of the people to keep and bear arms, shall not be infringed.
—Second Amendment,
Constitution of the United States of America

CHAPTER 17

"Keep Your F$#&ing Thoughts and Prayers..."

Washington DC

President Nancy Pillosi, the 46th POTUS, was a blessing for Americans. OK, she was a blessing for most sane rational Americans who believed that Donald J. Trimp had been a cancerous tumour of a president. By contrast, for that 22 per cent of America who still believed that Trimp was sent by God to MAGA, Nancy Pillosi was a hideous liberal she-witch, the devil incarnate, a female Antichrist sent to drag America from greatness into the fires of eternal damnation.

At least that was the opinion of Fox Entertainment's special guest, David Duke. He was pretty much foaming at the mouth when the host asked him about Nancy Pillosi's rise to the White House.

"Women should never have been allowed to vote, let alone hold political office," Duke was saying on Hanratty's show. He was dressed in the robes of the Grand Wizard of the Ku Klux Klan. "And now we have a smart-mouth, yappy white woman as president, and a Muslim female negro running to be our next president? Our forefathers would not be proud of how far we have fallen."

Trimp's three years of divisive and hateful politics had brutally divided the (previously) United States. During Trimp's brief reign of terror, Nazis, racists and just plain assholes had been encouraged (by the actions and example of their POTUS) to speak and act out their darkest hate-filled fantasies.

But Trimp's reign was clearly over, at least for those 78 per cent of Americans who could read the tea leaves, listen to logic, or admit the truth.

Pillosi's firm, fair, grandmotherly leadership was like a gentle, soothing, healing ointment on the grievous wounds of a nation. OK, on the wounds of 78 per cent of the nation.

Pillosi had fought for the people of San Francisco as a Congresswoman since 1987. During those 30-plus years, she represented her constituents with honesty and integrity. She had sponsored more bipartisan bills and legislation than any representative in US history. In 2006, she was elected by her peers in the Democratic Party as House speaker, the highest political office ever held by a female politician in America. Then she did it again. Following the 2018 midterms, she had again been elected as House speaker. Despite serving 33 years in the world's most brutal blood sport, Nancy Pillosi had very few enemies (for a politician) who hated her vehemently. Quite the opposite, many moderate Republicans thought highly of Pillosi:

"President Pillosi and I don't agree on many topics, but I consider her a dear friend and honourable colleague.

Although we play for opposite teams, Nancy Pillosi is living proof that politicians can comport themselves in a tough but fair and respectful manner. Don't be hatin', America. Give this lady a chance."–Warren Thatch, Republican senator, 1977- 2020.

By early April, the Federal Election Committee was revamped and restructured. The FEC's new composition was three representatives from each party, Republican, Democrat and Independent. By mid-April, there were Independent candidate names on every ballot for the upcoming election. Later in April, President Pillosi imposed sanctions on Russia for interference in elections in 2016 and 2018. The sanctions were also to be considered a deterrent to the 2020 elections.

The Republican primary was a bit embarrassing. All right, bigly embarrassing. During the debates, Sarah Palon, Steve Bannin and Mikki Haley were all trying to seduce the far-right voters with promises of nationalism along the lines of Trimp's "America First" campaign.

Jeb Busch, Marco Rubion and Todd Cruz–the "moderate' front runners–were seen as a less-dangerous option. Far-right nationalistic or Trimpanzee Republicans actually made up the majority of the party now. Most moderate or sane Republicans had left the party between 2017 to 2018. The Republicans who remained as proud members did so out of party loyalty, dogged determination or sheer blind stupidity.

The Washington Post editorial, May 3rd

"The Grand Old Party is now just old. It is filled with old people, clinging to older outdated ideals. A more fitting acronym for the party would be 'Grumpy Old

People.' The average age of its membership is 63. The GOP's moderate candidates—Busch, Rubion, Cruz—seem to quietly understand that their party is being lead to the slaughterhouse, but also that they are powerless to stop the procession. The far-right Republican candidates actually seem to believe that they can form the next government. Have stranger things happened in America? Yes. Remember when we elected Donald J. Trimp?"

The debate in the Democratic primaries was more reasonable and respectful. It was as if the Democratic party was mirroring the Independent candidates trying to run on facts, reason, love and hope rather than lies, division, fear and hate. It was a good attempt, but seen by many Americans as too little, too late. You could feel the change in the air. It was palpable.

In July, Mikki Haley won the Republican primary and chose Marco Rubion as her vice-presidential candidate. Republicans applauded the choice, mostly for having the courage to propose a young female candidate for president. Party analysts seemed hopeful that votes on the left would be split between Democrats and Independents, leaving all right-inclined voters to elect another Republican government.

A few days later, "Uncle" Joe Baden won the Democratic primary and, surprising none, selected young Jim Kennedy as his running mate. The Democratic party liked their chances. Both these candidates were well spoken and relatively scandal free.

America had three televised presidential debates, and three televised vice-presidential debates. In the first presidential debate, the moderator warned Mikki Haley twice not to interrupt other speakers. Much like her mentor, Trimp, she was unable to control herself, however, and had to be physically removed from the set. Suitably chastised, she behaved more admirably in the following two debates.

The Gallup polls taken after each debate had Michelle Oobima as the clear runaway winner, with "Uncle" Joe Baden in second and Mikki Haley a distant third. During the debates, Mikki tried to feed red meat to the old Trimp/GOP base on issues like gun control, women's rights over their reproductive organs, and religious freedom (to worship Republican Jesus.) All three issues backfired horribly, to the amusement of all (save the far-right Republicans.)

The VP debates were also very watchable. Marco Rubion was a good speaker with lots of experience (but his ties to Trimp and long service in the GOP was hurting him.) Jim Kennedy was the youngest candidate, had some experience as a representative, and was also a good speaker. Some people couldn't get past his last name, however, or the fact that he was yet another trust-fund millionaire politician for life.

Dwain John-Stone undeniably stole the show in the vice-presidential debates. He was remarkably well spoken and was able to articulate simple, achievable ways that America could meet the many challenges it faced. He was smart and very intelligent, but in a likeable way. (Smart people can be unlikeable if they rub our faces in how smart they are/stupid we are.) He was funny, open and honest. And he had recently been voted Sexiest Man in America. Americans seemed to like all those qualities and achievements, according to numbers in the polls.

Summer slowly turned to fall. The Republican candidates, in response to low polling numbers, resorted to vicious attack ads on their Independent and Democratic opponents. Semi-reluctantly, the Democratic Party candidates followed suit, attacking the Independents. Attack ads had always worked well in the past, right?

The Independent candidates did not respond in kind. They had agreed in their original party platform meetings on some simple common points.

Independent Party: Candidate Guidelines, Drafted Jan. 22, Montpelier VT

Independent candidates WILL NOT accept corporate donations. The reason why is in our name. How can we claim to be independent if you take money from a corporation?

Independent candidates MAY accept donations from private citizens up to $2,700.00 (Choose wisely. If you honestly need financial help to campaign, discuss with Finance HQ. We are running a campaign based on open, honest austerity. In every case, the LESS we spend, the MORE we all win.) Note: Republican and Democratic candidates can receive up to $970,000.00 per individual and corporate donations in accordance with FEC regulations. Good for them. Good for us. Americans are smart people. Explain these guidelines, then let them decide.

Independent candidates WILL openly track donations received as revenue. Travel, lodging, meals and campaign-related costs as expenses. See above. The LESS we spend as candidates, the MORE people will like it. Annex B has a recommended template we WILL all use. It will ensure we can present our finances to the public in a simple, understandable, consistent format.

Advertising: Independent candidates WILL NOT run attack ads against other candidates. A simple statement of fact where you stand on each issue is more effective. Independent candidates, SHOULD defend their views or provide a statement of facts if opponents make false claims against our candidates. Resist the urge to attack the other candidates. In so doing, our Independent candidates will maintain the moral and ethical high ground.

Independent candidates should be just that: independent. On a broad spectrum, candidates should support policy and legislation that benefits their constituents without harming other parts of the country or the global environment. Example: in 2017, the State of New York placed a ban on fracking, sacrificing significant short-term economic gain for long-term environmental health. Contrast this decision with Trimp's recent political support of "clean, beautiful coal." Which decision was more courageous? Which decision was short sighted or done for short-term political gain?

In September, the national security advisor briefed President Pillosi and the Senate that:

"Despite recent sanctions, Russian interference in the US electoral system was 'endemic, ongoing, persistent and concerning.' Social media platforms have multiple 'fake' or 'foreign' accounts aiming to influence American voters. Additionally, our voting machines are easily compromised, and election results can therefore be altered or amended by outside influencers."

The 2020 American election was being anticipated as the most dramatic, emotional and contentious in US history.

The new and revamped FEC reacted swiftly and appropriately. The government ordered social media platforms to verify accounts as actual people or delete them. Failure to comply resulted in heavy fines.

The new president took several more precautions to ensure that the election was run fairly, in accordance with principles long established in most democracies.

"There is no voting machine we can design that is both affordable and safe from hackers," Nancy Pillosi announced from the White House. "Therefore, we are returning to a hand counted paper ballot system. This system is more labour intensive but ultimately is tamper-proof and inexpensive. Additionally, early polls indicate that a record-high number of eligible voters intend to participate in this upcoming election. In the 2016 and 2018 elections, there weren't enough polling places to support the number of citizens who wanted to vote. Many people were turned away after midnight despite having waited five hours to vote. We anticipate a 40 per cent increase in voters for this election. The FEC, therefore, intends to double the number of polling places in every state and district in the USA. Additionally, more advance polling places and systems will be organized in order to manage the anticipated high voter turnout. We are going to need your help with this America. To volunteer, contact www.getoutandvote.

In October, anticipating record-high voter turnout and fearing potential violence (based on intelligence and recommendations from Homeland Security), President Pillosi reluctantly took the final step she deemed necessary to ensure a fair and safe election.

She requested 1,000 international UN election officials and 250,000 UN peacekeepers from Canada.

"She did what now?" Americans asked. "Did I hear that right?"

"The president requested 250,000 UN peacekeepers to augment security forces in the upcoming election." repeated the various media outlets.

This was not a popular request among the elderly, or hardcore lifelong Democrats or Republicans. It was far and away the most unpopular thing President Pillosi did during her brief presidency.

"This request to the UN for assistance is just unnecessary and embarrassing!" Mikki Haley shouted at President Pillosi on CNN. "This is the United States of America! We invented democracy and freedom! We ensure other countries have fair elections with good outcomes that we approve of. We are not a banana republic that needs international help to ensure a fair election!"

"Yes, we are, Ms. Haley," Nancy Pillosi responded calmly. "It hurts me to say it, but it's true." She spun in her chair to address the TV cameras and viewers at home. "Let's be honest with ourselves, America. We have, in fact, recently become a banana republic, and we do need international assistance to hold a safe and fair democratic election. Ms. Haley, have you forgotten the chaos of our past year already? Have you forgotten that 2.6 million

Americans were recently arrested and illegally incarcerated during peaceful demonstrations in accordance with our First Amendment Rights?"

Mikki Haley was poised to interrupt, but Pillosi hushed her.

"Have you also forgotten that there was significant foreign interference in our last two elections? Have you read the intelligence advisory that warns America does not have enough security forces to safeguard American citizens during this upcoming election? Have you read the multiple conspiracy theorists that are already planning to declare the election results as rigged unless their party forms government?" President Pillosi got angrier and more determined as she continued.

"Have you read the minority voter suppression reports from the last two elections, which clearly state that our electoral system suppressed the votes of 10 million Americans citizens? Have you already forgotten that a duopoly of Democrats and Republicans colluded for the last 150 years to ensure that America only ever had two choices? Are you aware that literally hundreds of fringe militia groups and armies of right-wing nutjobs are threatening to use violence to disrupt and suppress American citizens from voting in this election? Surely you've read the threats from thousands of people who said that they will do 'whatever is required' to re-establish Donald Trimp as POTUS?"

Mikki Haley couldn't give up without a fight. "None of these recent events justify you asking the UN to bring 250,000 armed soldiers from other countries into the United States of…"

"Armed? Excuse me?" President Pillosi interrupted indignantly. "Ms. Haley, they aren't going to be armed! These are peacekeepers, also known as UN observers. They are just coming to observe the election and help our military and security forces ensure an orderly election."

Mikki Haley was gobsmacked, unbelieving, incredulous. "This plan just keeps getting more ludicrous. What use are unarmed peacekeepers? And what government in its right mind sends unarmed soldiers into a potentially hostile…"

She let her statement trail off, realizing she had just portrayed her country as a place where you needed to carry a gun to vote.

President Pillosi could smell her opponent's blood in the water. "You were asking where these peacekeepers and election officials are coming from? Well, the peacekeepers are members of the Canadian military and Canadian police officers. And like I just said, they are coming as unarmed observers. The Canadian prime minister has asked that we just consider them as tourists with blue berets. The election officials, meanwhile, are coming from various countries all over the world. Most have recent experience in identifying threats to fair and impartial voting systems and providing low-cost viable alternatives to ensure a fair election takes place."

President Pillosi paused to clear her throat, and looked at America over her glasses, like a kindly grandma frankly explaining something embarrassing but quite essential.

"Folks, I never ever dreamed I would ever be the president of this great country. But now, under circumstances I never imagined possible, that I am the president for a few more months, it's my job to ensure that every eligible American citizen gets a chance to vote in a safe and fair election. I'm getting security alerts from all over our country that indicate Russian splinter groups are planning to interfere in our election again, and that multiple groups from the lunatic fringe here in America intend to use all means necessary to suppress voters. So, you might disagree with the steps I'm going to take to ensure a safe and fair election, but sometimes being a leader means making difficult decisions. And this is one of those times."

As promised, UN election officials from all over the globe arrived in early October. Some of them were experts who had discovered or implemented ways to safeguard elections from voter fraud or voter suppression of minorities. All of them were election officials in their own country. All of them completed a week-long training course run by the new Federal Election Commission which explained US voter eligibility and election rules. Each of the officials understood that they were in the USA to ensure an extra bipartisan set of eyes. Each of the UN officials understood their role was to identify potential threats to a fair election in accordance with US election rules. Each of them was paired with an American election official. Each UN election official wore a UN badge. After the first day, when a black female official from Cote d'Ivoire was nearly lynched in the Indianapolis airport, each was provided a full-time police escort.

On November 2-3, the Canadian peacekeepers started arriving. Many arrived in smaller towns and cities in groups of 12,18 and 24 in their snazzy new Beaver and Otter airplanes. Thousands more flew into regular airports on regular fights. Some arrived by boat, across rivers, lakes or bays that separated the two countries. In places like Derby Line, Vermont, they just marched across the border from Stanstead, Quebec. On arrival they were met by their American counterparts.

The deputy sheriff from Waco, Texas was not thrilled about having to escort Canadian peacekeepers. He was less thrilled when he saw them. He had spent three years in the US Army Reserve himself before becoming an officer of the law. He watched the Canadians with a practised eye while they waited for their backpacks on the luggage carousel. There was an Indian soldier with a turban, another native Canadian soldier with a long braid, people of every colour with a buncha different accents…

Every peacekeeper wore the Canadian camo-pattern military uniform, had a military issue backpack, a standard military first-aid kit, a UN badge and a UN blue beret. *Hijab or turban?* The most noticeable thing about these soldiers, to the deputy's eye, was what they didn't have. *They don't have guns?*

It all seemed quite unbelievable to the deputy. "Y'all really didn't bring guns?" he asked the Canadian soldier closest to him. He had been briefed that the peacekeepers would be unarmed, but it seemed very odd.

"We find that these work better, Sir," Pte. Gonzales said with a strong Latino accent, handing the deputy a dried flower. The deputy dropped it like she had handed him a rattlesnake.

"I'm so sorry," Fabiola responded sincerely, picking up the flower. "Do you have allergies?"

"Nnn…no, I just wasn't expecting a soldier to give me a damn flower," the older deputy blustered. "It ain't normal."

"I guess not," Pte. Gonzalez replied, giving the flower to an older lady who was looking curiously at the peacekeepers.

"Y'all got a lot of girls in your army," the deputy remarked to Pte. Gonzales, hoping to change the subject.

"Yes, we do," Pte. Gonzales replied.

The deputy seemed surprised by her accent. "You don't sound very Canadian," he said suspiciously, while reading her nametag. "And, now that I think of it, a lot of you people don't look very Canadian either."

"Really? What is a Canadian supposed to sound and look like?" she responded with a wry smile.

"Well, kinda like the people in Minnesota," the deputy replied.

Pte. Gonzalez smiled again. It was a very disarming smile. "We are a very diverse people, us Canadians. Now I'm a new Canadian, recently arrived from Guatemala, so not all my friends are gonna look and sound like me."

In spite of his preconceived ideas of why he wouldn't like the peacekeepers, the older deputy was being worn down by a full-on charm offensive.

In fact, 52 per cent of the recently expanded Canadian Forces were female, and 73 per cent of the peacekeepers selected for this mission were women.

"Girls are just less threatening than boys," Danni Grey Eyes had recommended to the minister of defence.

"Danni's right," a very pregnant Juliette Sparks added. "Some Americans are already resentful or embarrassed that UN peacekeepers are going to be observing this election. People that are upset or angry about that will be less upset or angry and less likely to lash out when they see a female soldier."

On November 4, 2020, the world watched with bated breath as Americans voted in historic numbers. Voter turnout by percentage of eligible voters had measured between 52 to 59 per cent since 2000. It was later determined that 2020's election had 84 per cent of eligible voter participation.

Multiple "patriotic" American individuals and groups like the KKK, the Three Per centers and their ilk showed up at polling places attempting to "discourage" people who didn't look, think or talk like them. They were met with solid, strong resistance from average citizens, who booed them, shamed them and videotaped them. At every polling station there were (at least) two American security officers and two Canadian peacekeepers.

"Remember what we discussed," Sgt.-Maj. Lee told her troops in Waco. "Just be pleasant and polite, walk up and down the lines, talk to people, introduce yourself, tell them where you're from. If anyone becomes aggressive to you or other citizens, don't try to be a hero. Just blow your whistle and your American counterpart will come running. Have fun and be safe."

In the months leading up to the election, many right-wing voters and groups promised a bloodbath if the Republican Party did not win the election.

On November 4 there were 435 gun-related deaths in the US. The national daily average of gun related deaths was 91. Considering that security officials had feared thousands of gun deaths on election day, they were pleasantly surprised with the final tally.

There were also thousands of physical assault charges registered that day. This was down significantly from what officials had feared several weeks before the election. Trimpanzees had been threatening a civil war since Trimp's arrest. The vast majority of instigators and perpetrators in both the gun violence and the physical assaults were right-wing white males over 40 years of age.

Seventy-seven per cent of the victims were visible minorities. The other 23 per cent were regular folks (or Canadian militia members) trying to prevent assault on visible minorities.

Much of the credit (albeit reluctantly) for a peaceful election was given to the Canadian peacekeepers. The Canadians, for their part, suggested that the credit should be given to their American federal, state and municipal counterparts.

On November 4, 2020, America elected its first Independent president. Analysts were quick to point out that America had also elected its first female president and its second black president named Oobima. Those same analysts also pointed out that Michelle Oobima was the first former FLOTUS to be elected POTUS. Still more analysts joked that Barrack Oobima was the first POTUS who would serve as…First Man of the United States? They all (Barrack included) agreed that FMOTUS was a clumsy acronym.

Independent representatives were elected in 223 districts, Democratic representatives in 176 districts and Republican representatives in 36.

The Senate seats were more evenly balanced. The Democrats held 41, the Independents won 40 and the Republicans had 19.

President-elect Michelle Oobima's acceptance speech at 2300 Eastern Standard Time was immediately proclaimed a masterpiece for the ages. Political pundits and historians worldwide placed it on the highest shelf possible, alongside Dr. Martin Luther King's *"I Have a Dream"* speech and Churchill's *"We Shall Never Surrender."*

Her words soared, and roared, and cried, and whispered. They healed, and challenged, and inspired, and united a people who had been brutally divided.

An uneasy calm seemed to settle over America.

Security officials at every level—FBI, CIA, Homeland, National Guard, state troopers and local police—were very concerned that radical militant groups or individuals still loyal to Trimp intended to cause chaos.

Arlington, Virginia

Seven days later, on November 11, Veterans Day, at the Tomb of the Unknown Soldier, president-elect Michelle Oobima and her husband were injured in an assassination attempt. There were 61 deaths, including seven members of the president-elect's security detail. There were 113 people injured.

The assassination attempt was carried out by six shooters and three driver accomplices who had strong links to the KKK and several other neo-Nazi groups. They smashed through multiple security checkpoints in three massive up-armoured trucks, and then opened fire on the crowd with rapid-fire high-capacity assault weapons. All nine of the assailants were shot by security forces and perished in the attempt.

They each left letters explaining why they were going to kill Michelle Oobima. The letters were filled with hate. Hate for Michelle and Barrack Oobima. Hate for black people. Hate for Muslims. Hate for liberals and socialists. Hate for the deep state. Hate for fake news. Hate for all the people who had betrayed Donald J. Trimp.

President-elect Michelle Oobima, the 47th POTUS, spoke to America the evening after the attack. Her hand was bandaged. She'd lost two fingers to a bullet. Her husband was in critical condition on life support.

She was resolute. Defiant. Compassionate. Majestic. Strong. Furious. Unwavering. Sad.

"I believe I speak for the majority of Americans when I say, this madness stops now. By all means, pray for and fondly remember those people who were killed or injured in this cowardly attack. But sending 'thoughts and prayers' alone are not a viable long-term solution for reducing gun violence in our country. We've been trying that for a long time and it's just not working."

Michelle paused, drew a deep breath, and looked directly into the camera.

"I promise you. NOW. IS. THE. RIGHT. TIME. to discuss common sense gun control in America."

About the Author

The author's early years were spent in three small but beautiful Southern Ontario communities: Paris, Huntsville and Springfield. As a teenager Mark survived (more or less) by working (more or less) as a : gravedigger, farmassist, greenskeeper, construction labourer, tree planter and bartender.

At the age of 20 – seeking some direction, adventure and hoping to stay out of trouble – Mark joined the Royal Canadian Navy. Over a 33 year career, the author was promoted through the ranks to Chief Petty Officer First Class, and then Commissioned From the Ranks to serve as a Logistics Officer. Mark served proudly in seven Ships, on various multinational deployments at sea, and on peacekeeping tours in Israel and Afghanistan.

While stationed in Halifax, he met his wife Elaine. They were married in 1986 and have 2 grown sons. Credit for any semblance of sanity or logical behavior exhibited by the author since 1986 is due entirely to the influence of the authors wife and children.

Mark is currently co-owner and operator of a large, green, delicious burrito bus. Come and see him if you want some amazing Mexican Fusion.

Mark and Elaine live in Dartmouth and Lake Charlotte Nova Scotia. They love to travel, so if you are planning to visit, or if he owes you money, give them a heads up.

Help.
We hope you enjoyed *The Mouse Who Poked an Elephant,* and *Mouse, Bear and Elephant Games.*
Could you please take a minute now to write a review on Amazon, Indigo, Goodreads or Bookbub?
We'd also appreciate if you could follow / like us on the following platforms:
www.mouseandelephantbooks.com
Facebook@mouseandelephantbooks
Twitter@mousephantbooks
Instagram@mousephantbook
We hope to launch Book Three in the series around July 2020.